The Last Witch beyond the Forest

To the Hill family,

I hope you enjoy the journey through the Forest, and beyond!

AJE

The Last Witch beyond the Forest

A. J. Birch

CONTENTS

Chapter 1

CONQUEST

Within a world not too different from ours, there was a place called the Kingdom of Selsior. And Selsior was the largest, and indeed the greatest, of the Fourteen Realms, which, together with lands in the north and the west, formed the Central Continent in The World.

For centuries, the Kingdom of Selsior lived in great prosperity. It was a very rich Kingdom, because it had been mining jewels in the north-east for many years – gemstones like emeralds, rubies, sapphires, and diamonds. Selsior had also been sitting on a huge goldmine, which made it even richer. In fact, there was so much gold that there were piles of it just sitting in some of the rooms in the Palace.

Selsior was a busy and bustling place – it was densely populated, with people living in rows and rows of terraced houses. Its people worked in the mines in the north-east, in the farms, fields and vineyards in the south, on the staff of the Palace in the west, and in many other places across the Kingdom. In the centre of Selsior, there was a great marketplace to which its people flocked to buy goods, like books and textbooks, pens, pencils and paper, bread and meat, wine and ales, and fruit and vegetables.

Selsior was renowned for its imposing castles, scattered around the Kingdom like guardians made of stone, protecting its people from danger. And there was a lot of danger around: on the northern border of the Kingdom there was an expansive forest.

Dwelling in the Forest were many potentially threatening creatures: Fairies (if there are a lot of them, they can be very scary and powerful); Bats (not normal-sized bats, but Bats which are very big, as tall as human children); Gnomes (they have been known to be aggressive); Giants (they can squash humans underfoot like we might squash ants [behaviour which is not recommended]); and the most notorious and dangerous of them all: Goblins (they desire power and wealth nearly as much as humans do, and they are willing to be violent to acquire such things).

Each of these kinds of creatures had established their own communities in the different sections of the Forest. The relations between these communities were difficult, to say the least, especially when the Goblins invaded and conquered the Forest after fleeing from the east. The Goblins had a lot of fun by being personally cruel to all of them, and also by playing them against each other. Distrust and suspicion were always in the atmosphere of the Forest.

But for decades, the castles had not been needed to stand guard over the Kingdom from the creatures of the Forest. This was because the Magical Folk from the Land of Zelnia, on the other side of the Forest, had been protecting the people of Selsior. This had been the case since the Alliance was struck between the Kingdom of Selsior and the Magical Folk of Zelnia sixty years ago.

The Goblins from the Forest had attacked the Kingdom, and after the King and Queen sent a distress signal to the lands around them, the Wizards and Witches had come to their rescue. So the King asked the Magical Folk if they would consider moving from the Land of Zelnia to the Kingdom of Selsior, in order to permanently protect its people from the creatures of the Forest, especially the Goblins. The Wizards and Witches accepted the King's invitation, so they flew over the Forest to make their home in Selsior and to defend it.

This alliance survived until that King of Selsior died and was replaced by his son. And the thing to know about this new King, along with his Queen, was that he had always felt that the Kingdom did not need the Magical Folk protecting it, and that it was strong and powerful enough to defend itself. They put all of their faith and trust in their Army, castles and money to keep any enemies of the Kingdom at bay. The King also planned to build a very tall and very long wall on the border of the Forest, to further shield the Kingdom from peril.

So as soon as this new King and Queen had acceded to the throne, the Palace decreed that from that point, magic was banned throughout the whole

Kingdom, and the Magical Folk were banished to the Land of Zelnia from where they came.

At first, the Magical Folk were angry with the King and Queen of Selsior, and were considering remaining in the Kingdom as an act of protest. But after many discussions and meetings, it was decided that they would indeed leave, much to their sadness and disappointment. The Magical Folk had rather liked their brief time in Selsior.

Over the next few days and weeks, the Wizards and Witches got on their broomsticks and flew over the Forest to Zelnia and re-settled there, living again in the houses that they had left behind. Once there, they grew crops in the fields and raised animals on the farms, recreating their idyllic community with each other. It reminded the Magical Folk of a simpler time, before they immersed themselves in the busyness of the greatest Kingdom in the Central Continent. And as time passed, they began to forget about their lives in Selsior.

Meanwhile, in Selsior, rumours had begun to spread that the creatures of the Forest were planning an attack. After all, they had discovered that the

Wizards and Witches were no longer the guardians of the land, and that the Kingdom was now vulnerable. So the King and Queen ordered soldiers from the Army to be posted on the borders of the Forest, to keep watch.

But one by one, all of the soldiers were killed during the night, only to be replaced by the Commander of the Army, who obstinately pretended that there was nothing wrong, claiming that his men were being killed by some mysterious illness or disease. Soldiers continued to be murdered in the night-time, so others started to abandon their posts. If they were caught, they were imprisoned for desertion.

One night, the Goblins of the Forest did indeed launch an assault on the Kingdom, after they had greatly multiplied and had marshalled a seemingly invincible force. The Goblins came with no great stealth or subtlety – they made terrifying screeching noises as they emerged out of the Forest, attacking anybody they encountered on their way, leaving devastation in their wake. The Goblins were met in battle by the Army of Selsior, which arrived on horseback. The Goblins eventually triumphed over the Army after a long, exhausting battle.

The Goblins overran the entire Kingdom, besieged all of its castles, and attacked the Palace, where the King and Queen were hiding. The King and Queen had soon realised they had terribly miscalculated by getting rid of the Wizards and Witches, whose presence in the Kingdom would have prevented such action being taken by the Goblins. They had made a serious mistake, and they were about to count the cost.

The Empress of the Goblins, their ruler, took over the Palace and declared a New Reign in the Kingdom of Selsior, having deposed the King and Queen. The Goblins seized them both, along with the Prince, who was a toddler at the time, and the royal family was placed in a dungeon. Trolls were put in charge of the dungeon, with the duty of providing the former rulers of the Kingdom with some food and water every day. The King and Queen daily feared that they were going to be poisoned by the food they were being given. And the only life the

Prince of Selsior had ever known was in captivity at the hands of the Trolls.

In order to assert the Goblins' supremacy, the Empress gave the Palace, and the moat surrounding it, a hideous makeover. The King and Queen's banners and flags were removed; the outer wall and the keep were painted black and dark green; the wooden drawbridge was replaced with a metal one, with daggers sticking out of it; and the water in the moat was replaced with green and gloopy slime. The transformation was a tragic and ghastly sight to behold.

The people of Selsior had to swear allegiance to the Empress as their ruler, and they were then made to work for the Goblins.

Some were in the Palace in the west, at the beck and call of the Empress, serving her every whim. Some were in the north-east, mining for gold and other jewels, now for the purpose of satisfying the Goblins' greed. Some were in the south, working in the farms, fields and vineyards, to provide the Goblins with food and wine. Craftsmen were given the job of carving and erecting statues of the

Empress of the Goblins, for everybody to see images of the person who ruled over them, if they ever needed to be reminded.

The Goblins recognised that their labour force had to earn money, because they needed to *survive* to work for them, but the wages were so low that the people of Selsior were barely getting by.

Meanwhile, on the other side of the Forest, in the Land of Zelnia, the number of Magical Folk decreased, as they died out or moved elsewhere. Most of the Wizards and Witches returned to the Ancient Woodland in the West, within the Enchanted Lands by the Serene Sea, where their ancestors had lived for millennia. But one Witch decided that she wanted to stay in the Land of Zelnia.

Years passed in the Kingdom of Selsior, and hope faded away as the people became accustomed to life under the Goblins' regime. There were a few skirmishes here and there between the people and the Goblins, but the people were always defeated and imprisoned for treason against the Empress. A whole generation of children grew up never knowing what it was like to be free.

So what were the people of Selsior going to do? Was there anything they *could* do? Was there enough rebelliousness in their hearts to put together a clever plan to defeat the Goblins once and for all? Or were they going to simply accept that this was the way life was now? That the Empress of the Goblins was their undisputed ruler? That the Kingdom of Selsior was never going to be free again?

Well, this is the story of a girl called Lily who came up with a clever plan, which was far better than anything anybody else could offer. And not only is this the story of a girl called Lily who *came up* with a clever plan to free the Kingdom of Selsior, this is the story of a girl called Lily who was committed to *carrying out* her clever plan to free the Kingdom of Selsior...

Chapter 2

LILY

The response to the attack was very quick and horrible. Lily saw the whole thing play out before her.

It was a dry but chilly autumn day, with the sun shining brightly between the clouds and a wind blowing from the east. Lily was walking around the marketplace when she spotted one man whispering in the ear of another, all the while looking at a group of Goblins which was marching through. She then found herself staring at the Goblins, realising that she had never stopped to really look at these creatures who ruled over her people. The Goblins were five foot six tall, with yellowy-green skin beneath armour as black as night, sharp claws on their bare hands and feet, fierce orange eyes, pointy ears, and beak-like noses.

The men Lily had spotted looked like they were plotting something, when all of a sudden, the whispering man charged at one of the Goblins and pushed him to the ground. He jumped on the Goblin and started hitting it. The other Goblins found this amusing for a while but then quickly grabbed the man and killed him with a sword, right there on the spot. There was a loud thump as the man's body collapsed heavily onto the ground.

Lily gasped at the speed and the savagery of the killing. Then a couple of other men charged the Goblins and attacked them with fists and feet. The first man grabbed the sword of the murdering Goblin and ran another one through with it, before being killed himself. The Goblins captured the second man, who had survived, and dragged him kicking and screaming to the filthy dungeons – a fate too terrible for Lily to imagine.

'This is what happens if any of you try to fight us!' one of the Goblins said, before joining the group on its way to the castle.

Lily ran back to her house, and her brown hair was blown into her face by the strong wind. When she got back, her mother Agatha was cooking in the kitchen. Seeing her mother was a comforting sight for Lily after the trauma of what she had just witnessed.

Lily was huffing and puffing so much that she thought she might run out of breath in her lungs. She never ran like that. There was no need to, as all sport was banned by the Goblins when they took over.

'Lily, are you all right?' Agatha asked anxiously.

'I just saw some men get killed because they attacked the Goblins,' Lily replied. 'It was so scary, the Goblins were so vicious and bloodthirsty, and they dragged the survivors off to the dungeons.'

'Oh, Lily, that must have been horrific to see,' Agatha said. 'I'm so sorry you were on your own. I should have gone with you.'

'I'll be all right,' Lily said. 'I just wish the Goblins weren't ruling over us. I wish Selsior was free.'

'So do I,' Agatha said. 'But it's been twelve years since the Goblins came from the Forest and took over the Kingdom. You know, I've quite forgotten what it was like to not be ruled by the Goblins.'

'It's all *I've* ever known,' Lily said contemplatively.

'I know,' Agatha said. 'And I'm sorry that my generation wasn't able to provide a better life for yours.'

Agatha gestured for Lily to come over to her. Lily did so and her mother wrapped her arms around her shoulders. Agatha stroked Lily's hair and kissed her on the head. Lily looked up at her mother and her eyes seemed even bluer to Agatha than they normally were.

Lily looked very much like her mother, and everybody thought so. They both had dark brown hair and piercing blue eyes, which was a rare combination; and Agatha looked young for her age while Lily looked older than she was, which was eleven-years-old.

Lily's siblings, on the other hand, both looked like Lily's father, Benjamin, who was tall, big-bellied, and bald except for the grey hair on the sides of his head. Now you are probably wondering how *children* could possibly look like that, but facially, Benjamin and his two youngest did indeed look very similar. They were Edwin, who was nine-years-old, and Hilary, who was seven-years-old. Edwin was tall for his age, with brown longish hair and hazel eyes (eye-colour which he shared with Benjamin), while Hilary was about the usual size for her age, with long brown hair and the same hazel eyes as her father and her brother.

'Isn't Dad back from the mine yet?' Lily asked her mother.

'No, not yet,' Agatha replied. 'He and your uncle are going around inviting the men of the Kingdom to a meeting.'

'A meeting about what?' Lily asked.

'I'm not entirely sure,' Agatha admitted. 'Why?'

'Just wondering,' Lily said. 'But how are they going to have a meeting when all gatherings are forbidden by the Goblins?'

'I don't know,' Agatha said. 'But your dad and your uncle are very determined to have this meeting with the men of the Kingdom.'

'Just the men?' Lily enquired.

'Yes, just the men,' Agatha responded clearly.

Lily did not say anything else after that. She went to her bedroom (which was on the same floor; Lily's house was what we would call a bungalow) and closed the door. She got out a book from under her bed and opened it up on her pillow. It was called *The History of the Kingdom of Selsior, the Forest, and the Land of Zelnia, from the 1st Era to the Present Day*, and it was a large blue hardback book, the largest and heaviest in Lily's collection.

Lily was an avid reader, with a massive bookshelf, although the bookshelf was not big enough to contain all the books Lily had. Even after the conquest of Selsior by the Goblins, books had been written and sold in the marketplace, but as with everything, the sales of the books did not profit the authors very much at all because a very large percentage of the money went to the Goblins, mostly to the Empress herself.

Lily read fairy tales, children's stories, fantasy books, history books, and many other types of book. She loved everything about books – the way they felt, the way they smelt, the stories they told or the information they imparted. For Lily, there was nothing in The World quite like books. They gave her a warm feeling inside.

Lily had bought the book currently resting on her pillow six months ago in the marketplace, with pocket money that she had been saving for a while. Benjamin always wanted to give his three children a little bit of pocket money each month, despite his small income.

The writer of the book was an historian and author called Stuart of the Deep Dene, a secluded valley in the far north. During his travels, the author had found a magical walking stick that made him invisible, which enabled him to do his research in the places where people are not normally permitted to go.

Lily started to re-read passages from the book. She read about the origins of civilisation in the lands; how the Magical Folk emigrated from the West; the creation of the Fourteen Realms; the rise of Selsior as the greatest kingdom; the creatures setting up their different societies in the Forest, and many other things – all the way through to the section about the sole remaining Witch in the Land of Zelnia.

Lily read of beautiful weddings, sombre funerals, miraculous births, extravagant coronations, powerful spells, magical duels, epic battles and crusades, and apparently endless feuds and wars, all told in prose, poetry or song. Towards the back of the book, there were several maps detailing the geography of Selsior, the Forest, and Zelnia, as well as the lands surrounding them.

Time passed very quickly as she flipped through the pages of her book. This was why Lily was so surprised when her mother's call came from the kitchen: 'Lily! Dinner!' Lily then looked outside her window and saw that it was dark already. She ran out of her bedroom and into the kitchen, where Edwin and Hilary were already sat at the table, holding their cutlery in preparation for their evening meal.

Lily was sometimes jealous of her siblings' naïve approach to life. They did not talk about the Goblins or ask questions about why life was the way it was. They woke in the morning, ate breakfast, had a few lessons at home, ate lunch, played games, ate dinner, read stories, and went to bed. Lily, on the other hand, always felt like she had the weight of the world on her shoulders, like it was her responsibility to do something about the plight of the Kingdom of Selsior. She felt it in her bones.

'Is Dad still not home?' Lily asked as she sat down at the kitchen table and picked up her knife and fork.

'No, he is not,' Agatha responded. 'We are going to have dinner without him. He will eat when he gets home.'

'I hope he is all right,' Lily said.

'Yes, he is perfectly all right,' Agatha said. 'Like I said, he is having a meeting with some of the other men in the Kingdom. That is all. We, meanwhile, are going to eat!'

'Hooray!' Edwin said cheerfully.

'We love food,' Hilary said.

Agatha now served up the meal and they sat eating. The food was delicious. It was slices of chicken and gammon with chips and salad, with a dollop of tomato sauce for good measure.

'Edwin, do you want to tell Lily about what you were learning this morning?' Agatha asked.

'Yes, all right,' Edwin said. 'I learned how to do long division, and I learned about the Continental Wars of the 24th Era. The wars happened when the Kingdom of Gorex declared war on Selsior, and all of the other twelve Realms chose a side.'

'Oh, yes, I remember learning about that,' Lily said. 'That period is very interesting, Edwin. Well done.'

'I'm looking forward to learning more tomorrow,' Edwin said.

'And Hilary, what did you learn?' Agatha asked.

'Um, I learned some of the eight times table,' Hilary said, 'and I learned about the Magical Folk and their history and stuff, then I did some flute exercises.'

'Oh, brilliant,' Lily said. 'That also sounds very interesting. And I'm glad to hear that you're still challenging yourself with your flute-playing.'

Although she was listening to, and indeed responding to, what her brother and sister were saying, Lily devoured her dinner speedily.

'Goodness me!' Agatha said. 'You must have been very hungry!'

'Oh, yes, I was,' Lily said. 'It was very tasty, Mum. That's why I ate it so quickly. You're the best cook in The World.'

'Ah, well, thank you, Lily,' Agatha said. 'I aim to please!'

'Can I be excused?' Lily asked, trying to sound as lovely and polite as she possibly could.

'What about dessert?' Agatha queried.

'Yes, what about dessert?' Hilary repeated.

'Dessert is the best bit!' Edwin said ecstatically.

'I'm full already, thank you,' Lily said. 'But I may have some dessert later, if that is all right?'

'Yes, it's chocolate brownies so I'll keep yours in the tin until you want it,' Agatha said. 'If Edwin doesn't eat it!'

Edwin licked his lips at the prospect of eating Lily's chocolate brownie as well as his own.

'Great, thank you, Mum!' Lily said, standing up from her seat.

'You're not up to anything, are you Lily?' Agatha asked.

'No, of course not!' Lily said chirpily, before escaping to her bedroom.

Once back in her bedroom, Lily thought about what she was about to do. Should she do it? Should she risk her life, and (more importantly) risk the lecture by her parents if they ever found out? But Lily always thought about the bigger picture, about what the real priority was, and she now thought about what she could achieve by doing what she was planning to do.

Lily grabbed her dark grey cloak off the hook on the back of her bedroom door. She then walked to her bed, closed the book on her pillow and picked it up. She went towards the window and opened it upwards. The book felt as heavy as a bag of bricks, and as Lily dropped it out of the window, it landed with such a thud that she was sure her mother would have heard it. But when no sound from the kitchen came, Lily climbed out of the window and pulled it down so there was a gap of just an inch. She picked up the book and quietly walked away, checking there were no Goblins nearby watching her.

When her mother told Lily that her father and her uncle were having a meeting for all of the men of the Kingdom, Lily knew there was only one place in Selsior large enough to hold such a big meeting: the Great Hall.

The Great Hall was an enormous stone building in the eastern end of the Kingdom, which had been used for centuries to celebrate important weddings and births, to host important funerals, to hold awards ceremonies, and to put on theatre and music performances – all before the Goblins took control of course. Ever since the invasion, the hall had been abandoned and it had fallen into a state of decay. Benjamin and Agatha used to tell their children such dazzling stories of the events that had been held there, and Lily was sad about the state in which she found it now.

Lily did not know how her father and her uncle had managed to invite so many men to this meeting, let alone how so many had been able to leave their houses or places of work and get inside without being detected by the Goblins. Lily remembered that there had been mentions of the Goblins getting complacent, having occupied the Kingdom of Selsior for such a long time. Maybe this was why Lily's father and her uncle had mustered the courage to organise such a risky meeting.

Lily's confusion continued as she too managed to creep in to the meeting without any trouble at all – her dark-coloured cloak helping her to avoid being seen. The meeting was being lit by a few lanterns and by candlelight, casting silhouettes of all the men upon the grimy walls. Lily walked cautiously towards the huddled mass of men, both young and old, which was encircling two men: Lily's father, Benjamin, and Lily's uncle, Simon. Her uncle looked very much like her father – he was tall, big-bellied and bald too, with the same hazel eyes.

The men in the meeting were taking turns to voice their opinions. While one or two were allowed to speak freely, others were shouted down as soon as their opinions apparently sounded too controversial or just downright stupid.

'What I've always wanted to know is why the other thirteen Realms haven't come to our aid,' one man said.

'We could never get a message out to them,' Simon answered. 'The Goblins stopped all communications with the other Realms.'

'Do you mean they don't even know we were invaded?' the man asked in disbelief.

'They don't know,' Simon said grimly.

'They wouldn't come to our aid anyway,' another said, 'not after the Continental Wars in the 24th Era.'

'What happened in the Wars was not our fault,' another said. 'We were attacked and we defended ourselves. That is all.'

The relationships between the Fourteen Realms had a very long and complex history. Although they shared the same landmass, they did not get on particularly well. They had been constant rivals, if not enemies in wars. The Kingdom of Selsior was the greatest of the Fourteen Realms, as has been mentioned, but this greatness did not just happen – it was won through blood, sweat and tears over many centuries. And the other Realms were inevitably very jealous of Selsior.

But the relationships were *so* bad that the other Realms were not even aware that Selsior had been taken over by the Goblins of the Forest on its northern border, as they did not keep in contact with each other. Even if the other Realms had heard that Selsior had been invaded, it was doubtful indeed that they would have actually come to its aid.

'I don't care about the other thirteen Realms!' one man said very loudly. 'I don't care what they are and are not doing. The real question is: how can *we* win back our Kingdom and get rid of these Goblins?'

'We all know the only way to beat them is with military force,' another said. 'We need to arm ourselves, we need to somehow get our hands on swords and shields, on bows and arrows, and we need to fight them!'

'How are we going to get our hands on weapons?' a man asked impatiently.

'I heard that when we were invaded, some of the soldiers in the Army of Selsior buried their weapons on the northern border, to stop the Goblins getting their hands on them,' an older man said.

'That's simply ridiculous!' another man said dismissively. And his dismissing of the man's suggestion paved the way for a whole barrage of angry rebuttals:

'That's an old wives' tale!'

'That story has just been invented to cast blame on the soldiers and make out that they were cowards!'

'Can you justify that allegation?'

'They would never have neglected their duty!'

'There is absolutely no way that the soldiers would have given up their weapons instead of meeting the Goblins in battle,' one man said, who was a veteran soldier himself, proud of some of the things he had done in the Continental Wars, but ashamed of many others.

'Well, why don't you look for them instead of ignoring the story?' the older man replied, before folding his arms.

'But that's all it is: a story,' the veteran said defensively.

'Enough of this,' Simon said, sighing. 'We are not here to argue among ourselves, we are here to discuss a plan to take back our Kingdom.'

'What about enlisting the support of the creatures of the Forest?' one young man said. 'The Fairies, the Bats, the Gnomes and the Giants? They hate the Goblins just as much as we do. They would want to help us.'

'The creatures of the Forest are not our allies,' an older man said. 'They are dangerous, devious, and not to be trusted. We cannot go asking for their support. That would be crazy.'

'I don't hear anyone else coming with up any clever ideas...' the young man said despondently.

After that last comment, there was silence for a few moments. Lily saw this as her one opportunity, and she did not want to squander it.

'I have an idea,' she said quite quietly, with her book by her feet.

'Who said that?' one man asked.

'It was me,' Lily said. 'Lily, the eldest daughter of Benjamin and Agatha.'

'Lily!' Benjamin yelled, coming to find her. 'What *are* you doing here?'

'Mum told me you were having a meeting with the men of the Kingdom and I wanted to see what it was about,' Lily said.

'Does your mother know you're here?' Simon asked.

'No, she doesn't,' Lily answered. 'I snuck out, if you must know.'

'Lily...' Benjamin said, disappointed.

'Dad, I have an idea about how to take back the Kingdom,' Lily said.

'Oh, do tell(!)' a man said from the back of the assembly.

'We should not appeal to the other members of the Fourteen Realms, or to the creatures of the Forest, but to the Land of Zelnia, on the other side of the Forest,' Lily said assertively. 'That is where the solution to our crisis lies.'

'That's an absurd proposition, little girl,' the veteran soldier said rudely, who could not really believe the men had even given this youngster the time of day.

'Why?' Lily asked, standing her ground. 'Why is it absurd?'

'We all know the Magical Folk are long gone,' the veteran said. 'Why would they stick around? What is there to stay for?'

'Not all of them are gone,' Lily said.

'What do you mean?' Benjamin asked.

'Most of the Magical Folk have left, yes,' Lily said. 'But one of them remained. A Witch. She chose to stay in Zelnia.'

'But why?' Benjamin asked. 'Why would one choose to stay when all of the others have gone? I don't understand it.'

'I'm not *completely* sure why this Witch stayed,' Lily said, 'but I think she would want to help us, if we asked her.'

'After the way we treated her kind?' another man chimed in. 'Not likely.'

'Well, we won't be sure until we ask her, will we?' Lily said irritably.

'This is all nonsense!' bellowed the veteran. 'We don't need these fairy tales from the past to beat the Goblins; we need weapons and soldiers to take them on. Those things are the only way to win freedom for Selsior!'

'I'm sorry, Lily, but the gentleman is right,' Benjamin said. 'We can't rely on some Witch who may or may not still be living in the Land of Zelnia. We need an army. And we need it now.'

'Find those swords buried on the northern border', said the man who had mentioned the weapons originally. 'Then you'll have a chance of victory. Mark my words.'

That was pretty much the end of the meeting, except for a short discussion about how they might take on the Goblins. Lily was disappointed that the assembly had not wanted to heed her advice at all. These men only wanted to take up swords, charge at the Goblins and meet them in battle. Lily also had the telling-off of a lifetime to look forward to, once her father had marched her home.

'What were you thinking going out in the dark? Going to a secret meeting of the men of the Kingdom? Risking being caught by the Goblins? Risking exposing the meeting to the Goblins?' All of these questions were asked by Benjamin in quick succession, not letting Lily get in any kind of answer.

'And I can't believe you just snuck out of the house! After dinner, you waltzed back to your room, you shut the door and you climbed out of your window,' Agatha said, unable to comprehend her daughter's behaviour.

'I know what I did, Mum,' Lily said.

'Well, what do you have to say for yourself?' Agatha asked, crossing her arms.

'I wanted to contribute to any meeting about how to free Selsior. I've read this book,' Lily said, pointing to the book which again was sat at her feet.

'What book?' Agatha asked.

'This book,' Lily said, pointing at the book another time.

Agatha cast her eyes down at the book and read out the title: '*The History of the Kingdom of Selsior, the Forest, and the Land of Zelnia, from the 1st Era to the Present Day.*'

'Yes,' Lily said. 'And it explains that there is one Witch left in the Land of Zelnia–'

'I don't want to hear all this stuff again, Lily,' Benjamin said. 'Please just go to your room.'

'But, Dad, I...' Lily pleaded.

'Now,' Benjamin said bluntly.

Lily picked up her book and walked to her bedroom. She slowly closed the door behind her, and locked it. Once she put her book back under her bed, Lily lit the candle on her bedside table, lay down on her bed, and sobbed.

When Lily had composed herself, she got her book out from under her bed once again, and started reading some more passages. She was looking for any bits of information that she might have missed when she was reading it before – anything she could use to bolster her argument for travelling through the Forest and appealing to the Witch in the Land of Zelnia. She read every paragraph twice and looked at each of the footnotes, like a detective scrutinising documents during an investigation.

After a while, Lily was so tired that she realised she had to get some rest. So she returned the book to its normal position under her bed, blew out her bedside candle, and fell asleep, thinking about, then dreaming about, the Witch residing in Zelnia, and all of the creatures in the Forest that stood between the Kingdom of Selsior and its salvation.

Chapter 3

DISSENT

The weapons were indeed found – buried underground on the northern border, on the edge of the Forest – in the middle of the previous night. There were swords, daggers, bows and arrows, axes, and spears. The man who had told the group about the rumoured hidden swords was duly vindicated, and he was failing to not look smug.

The old veteran soldier, on the other hand, was incredibly disappointed by the discovery, as it meant that the soldiers who should have been bearing arms in the defence of the Kingdom had chosen instead to surrender their weapons, and bury them in the ground beneath their feet. He said bitterly that those men should be found and executed for desertion – cowardice must never be tolerated.

In pitch black, the men had dug up the swords and taken them back to the Great Hall. They were all surprised that they had not encountered any Goblins at all. While they were going about their search, the men half-thought that they would be caught – it was just a matter of time. But they were willing to risk being caught in the pursuit of an opportunity to take on the Goblins.

But the Goblins felt that they had now suppressed all pockets of resistance across the land, so they need not patrol the roads and streets of the Kingdom all of the time. After all, the Goblins had repeatedly shown how ruthless and brutal they were towards anybody who dared to resist them. The people were not going to cause any more trouble, were they?

Lily was again walking through the marketplace when she saw the battle. She had been looking all around the marketplace for the seller of her book, to see if there was a second edition of it on sale, with amendments or more up-to-date information within its pages (that the Witch had recently left Zelnia, for example!). Alas, she had not found him anywhere.

But what Lily did find was her uncle Simon making a *big* mistake. They had gathered in the Great Hall and prepared a strategy for their attack on the Goblins. Arming themselves with swords was the first glimmer of hope in years, as they now had a chance of inflicting some damage on their Goblin masters. However, the strategy was not one that had been thought through very well. Military tactic was not these men's strong suit, but they had impulsive recklessness in spades.

The men were hiding the swords under their cloaks. And when the right opportunity seemed to arise, Simon led this ragtag army into the Goblin military squad that was marching through the marketplace towards the Palace of the Empress.

The battle initially looked like it was going the way of Simon's army, but Lily quickly realised that it was simply the element of surprise that had given the men of Selsior their early advantage. Lily watched in horror as the Goblins began to win the battle by slicing and hacking at their opponents, until there was a heap of bodies on the blood-stained ground. Some of the men were still alive and Lily put her hand over her mouth as she saw her uncle being hauled away by his ankles, along with a few of his fellow soldiers.

Lily knew exactly where they were heading: into the castle dungeons to be watched over by the bad-tempered Trolls. She had heard that some of the prisoners had simply *disappeared* after being locked up by the Goblins. There were stories being circulated that the Trolls got peckish and gobbled up the inmates who were particularly noisy and obnoxious, and that their ghosts would haunt the cells and corridors of the castle for all eternity.

The Goblins got very cruel after the battle that morning. They were angry with themselves for getting complacent in their ruling of the people. Except for the very small scuffle that Lily had seen the day before, there had been no rebellion from the people for years. So the Goblins had assumed that by and large, the people had adjusted so much to being ruled by the Goblins that they would not attack them. But they had been wrong to assume that – there were flames of dissent still burning away in the hearts of men, threatening to become a wildfire of mutiny.

The Goblins in charge of the mines became harsher with their batons and whips; the thugs patrolling the Kingdom pushed and hit people walking past them, completely at random and completely unprovoked; and the Empress of the Goblins was even more unpleasant towards the people serving her in the Palace.

But the men of the Kingdom caught a break when the entire Goblin population went to the Palace one night to celebrate the twelfth anniversary of the Goblins' capture of Selsior. The Empress was holding a lavish banquet, hosting a boisterous party, and was going to give a stirring speech about the magnificence of the Goblins, a speech she had compelled one of her human servants to help write and perfect.

So another meeting was called in the Great Hall. Benjamin was leading this one on his own, now that Simon was in a dungeon. His brother was more of a natural leader, so Benjamin found the prospect daunting. And Lily was not helping particularly.

'I'm going with you to the meeting,' Lily said directly.

'No, you're not,' Benjamin said, just as directly, before moving away from his daughter.

He underestimated his daughter's persistence: 'Dad, the men have to know what is in this book,' Lily said, while nodding towards the book she was holding under her right arm. She was trying not to let it show that it was a strain holding such a weighty object.

'There's nothing in that book that can help us!' Benjamin said.

'What other options do you have, Dad?' Lily asked. 'Uncle Simon tried fighting them and that didn't work, did it?'

'It will if we try again with more of a strategy next time,' Benjamin said.

'No, it won't,' Lily countered. 'The Goblins are too many, and too good at fighting. Trust me, the answer is in this book, the answer is on the other side of the Forest.'

'Lily, I...,' Benjamin began.

'Dad, just let me make my case, for goodness' sake!' Lily said rather angrily. 'Allow me to make my case properly, then I will never interfere in your affairs or attend a meeting ever again.'

Benjamin sighed. Then he looked at Lily in a different way: rather than seeing her as bothersome and meddlesome, he saw her as clever, knowledgeable and brave. His oldest daughter was just trying to help, and perhaps the men in the meeting *could* benefit from what she had read in this book?

'All right,' Benjamin said as he scratched his bald head. 'You can come with me. Just this once.'

'Thank you, Dad,' Lily said.

'I will have to clear it with your mother,' Benjamin said. 'And she won't be happy about it!'

Lily smiled as her father went off to negotiate with his wife. Maybe she was going to be able to get through to the men of the Kingdom now. After the defeat of her uncle and his army, they would surely be more willing to listen to alternative options.

'You know what we have to do: we must appeal to the magical community on the other side of the Forest, in the Land of Zelnia...'

If only you could have seen Lily's face at that moment! For that statement was not being made by Lily, but by a man in the meeting who Lily recognised from the last meeting. He was suggesting the idea as if it had never been mentioned before.

'Yes, that does seem to be the answer,' another said.

'I think you'll find that I recommended that course of action before,' Lily said crossly.

'Yes, Lily did actually say that at our previous meeting,' Benjamin said, helpfully backing up his daughter, who smiled at him.

However, both Lily and Benjamin were drowned out by the clamour of voices that erupted after the man had made the suggestion. The men all spoke over each other, which meant that nobody's voice was clearly heard. Lily could only watch as the men all pointed fingers at one another, shook their heads, and waved away anyone who disagreed with their own point of view.

Benjamin walked with obvious anger towards a wooden table at the side of the Great Hall, raised his hand, and slammed a clenched fist down so loudly that the whole meeting came to an abrupt silence. Lily was proud of her father for bringing the rowdy assembly of men to order so effectively.

'Lily?' Benjamin said. 'Do you want to explain *your* suggestion?'

Lily smiled again at her father, picked up her book, and walked over to join Benjamin at the table. She gently put the book down on the table, then turned around to face the group of men.

'Far away in the north,' Lily began, 'on the other side of the Forest, is the Land of Zelnia, the homeland of the Magical Folk for centuries. You should all know the history: they moved to Selsior to protect the people from the creatures of the Forest, then twelve years ago, magic was banned in the Kingdom and the Wizards and Witches were expelled. Over the last few years, most of the Magical Folk have moved to the West but one Witch chose to stay.'

'You mean there's only *one* left?' interrupted one man.

'Yes,' Lily said. 'There is only one. The author of my book believes that the Witch is very old and towards the end of her life. So we have to speak to her as soon as we can.'

'Who wrote this book?' another man asked. 'Where did you get it from?'

'The author researches and writes about the history and culture of different places across The World,' Lily said. 'I bought it in the marketplace.'

'But what I just don't get is why she decided to stay when none of the others has,' yet another man said.

'The author doesn't actually say *why* the Witch stayed,' Lily said. 'He might not know – he might not have necessarily spoken to the Witch herself, he will have just heard about her continued presence in Zelnia through his research. I imagine that's the case anyway.'

'So why do *you* think this Witch stayed?' the same man asked.

'Well, I believe the Witch is staying in Zelnia so she can help us someday,' Lily responded. 'She is simply waiting for us to ask her, waiting for our cry for help.'

Lily was aware that they seemed to be repeating themselves from the previous meeting. But something had changed in the reception to what she had to say. The men assembled were not brushing it aside – they were actually listening this time, and asking reasonably sensible questions. There was no doubt that their attitude had altered because Lily's father had instructed them to listen, but Lily also commanded their continued attention.

'So what are you actually proposing?' a man asked, while looking puzzled in Lily's direction. He could not really believe he was asking an eleven-year-old girl to explain the plan which she had devised to rescue the Kingdom of Selsior. He was baffled by the whole thing to be honest.

Lily stood up straight, exhaled, and said with much self-confidence: 'What I am proposing is that a group ventures through the Forest to the Land of Zelnia, in order to speak to the Witch and ask that she help the people of Selsior against the Goblins. That is the *only* way to save our homeland.'

The men assembled in the Great Hall were taken aback by the confidence and courage that Lily exuded in front of a group of men much older than her. They seemed to finally understand that she truly had the right answer, the answer they had been seeking ever since the Goblins had stamped their vicious authority on the Kingdom.

'Thank you, Lily,' Benjamin said, indicating that his daughter could now return to the back of the crowd. But Lily stayed put right beside her father.

'Your daughter is correct, Benjamin,' one man said. 'That *is* the only way. Some of us will have to go through the Forest to ask for the Witch's help.'

'Yes,' Benjamin said in agreement. 'We will send a group to accomplish this mission.'

'But who is going to go on this hazardous journey?' asked the man. 'Must I remind you that not only are there Goblins patrolling the edge of the Forest, but once you get into the Forest itself, there are other treacherous creatures: Fairies, Bats,

Gnomes, Giants... How are we going to protect ourselves from those things?'

'We will think about each of these factors when the time comes,' Benjamin said. 'Let's not get ahead of ourselves.'

'Well, who's going to go?' barked one of the older men present. 'Who's going to stand up, be brave and embark on this operation to liberate our once-great Kingdom?'

After this aggressive outburst, Lily's voice came like a whisper: 'According to my book, the Magical Folk tended to respond most to children, because of their open-mindedness to magic and to the world beyond their own. Perhaps this would be the case with this Witch?'

'You're talking about sending *children*?' asked one man incredulously. 'Children *your* age?'

'Yes, I am,' Lily replied.

'It is preposterous to send children into such terrible danger,' another man said.

'Yes, preposterous,' a few men said concurrently.

'No, no, wait,' Benjamin said. 'Lily has been right about things so far. I think we'd agree on that. If that is what this expert historian and author says, then that is advice we must heed. Only children can get the Witch on our side. So we will select brave young people, no younger than eleven-years-old, who will be prepared, and equipped, to trek through the Forest, to the Land of Zelnia on the other side, to ask this Witch to come to our aid. It is decided.'

At that very moment, the men keeping watch outside the Great Hall came rushing in, panting. They had fear and anguish clearly upon their faces. One of the men was so worn out and distressed that he could not even speak.

'We've got a message that the Goblins' anniversary feast is over!' the other man shouted. 'They're coming out of the Palace now!'

'This meeting is adjourned!' exclaimed Benjamin urgently. 'Everybody get out of here now!'

It was absolute chaos as the men frenziedly rushed to the door and scarpered. Benjamin grabbed Lily's hand and ran out of the Great Hall. Lily had just got the book in her grip when her father took hold of her. She definitely did not want that getting into the hands of the Goblins.

Agatha gasped as the door to the house was burst open and was then slammed shut. Benjamin looked through the letterbox to check that no Goblin had been following him and Lily. Lily, meanwhile, clutched her book to her chest and looked up at her father.

'Are you all right?' Agatha asked.

'Yes, we are all right, Agatha,' Benjamin said. 'The meeting just ended rather, uh, abruptly.'

'You'd better not be endangering our daughter, Benjamin...' Agatha said.

'Dad, I want to talk more about the plan,' Lily interjected.

'I know you do, Lily,' Benjamin said. 'But I am very hungry, very thirsty and very tired. So I'm going to eat some supper, have a drink, and go to bed.'

'Dad, I'm going to go through the Forest to Zelnia to speak to the Witch,' Lily said with conviction in her voice.

'What?' Benjamin exclaimed, looking at Agatha, who was equally shocked. 'No, no. Look, I'm very grateful for the contribution you brought to the meeting and the influence you had in the final decision, but you are not going on the journey yourself.'

'Why not?' Lily asked.

'There are certain things that girls don't do in our Kingdom, Lily,' Benjamin answered.

'Like what, Dad?' Lily asked.

'Like embarking on dangerous missions through a treacherous forest, full of hostile and scary creatures,' Benjamin replied.

'The author of my book says that the creatures are not actually that hostile,' Lily said. 'They were victimised and mistreated by the Goblins just as badly as we are now.'

'Do you know what those creatures are?' Benjamin asked in disbelief. 'Fairies, Bats, Gnomes, Giants! All of them are dangerous and happen to not be very fond of humans...'

'But all of them are united with us in hating the way the Goblins treat other kinds!' Lily said. 'The creatures will let us pass if we tell them what our ultimate goal is – the downfall of the Goblins.'

'They won't listen to any explanation,' Benjamin said. 'They will only let the young men pass when they are threatened with swords and daggers.'

'You know that's not true,' Lily said. 'We must talk things through, instead of threatening anyone or anything about which we don't know, or, more likely, of which we are *scared*.'

'I'm not talking about this anymore, Lily,' Benjamin said. 'I've made up my mind: you are not going. End of discussion.'

'But it was my book that supplied the information you needed to decide the course of action,' Lily said.

'Yes, and I am thankful for that,' Benjamin said, 'but the journey itself is too dangerous.'

'But I am courageous enough to go on the journey!' Lily cried. 'Don't you approve of that?'

'Of course I do,' Benjamin said, 'but the mission is still too perilous for you to actually embark upon. We will be choosing some of Selsior's fittest, bravest boys to achieve the task. Now *that* really is the end of the discussion.'

Benjamin walked off to the kitchen and made himself a beef sandwich. Agatha went to put her arm around her daughter, but as she did so, Lily stormed off to her bedroom and slammed the door behind her. Lily hoped her parents had got the hint that she was a *bit* annoyed.

Lily was sat on her bed, reading her book once again, when her parents came in. She ignored them and continued reading. Agatha sat on the bed beside Lily. Benjamin remained standing, with his arms crossed.

'Lily, I know you're upset,' Agatha said, stroking her daughter's hair. 'I know you want to do your bit and play your part in this mission, but it is just too dangerous.'

'If I hear someone tell me that one more time...!' Lily exclaimed.

'But it's true,' Agatha said.

'I know it's true, but I am prepared to go through dangerous places and meet *potentially* dangerous creatures in order to save my homeland,' Lily said.

'But *we're* not prepared to let you do that,' Agatha said.'

'I have read all about the creatures of the Forest and about the Witch in the Land of Zelnia, in this book,' Lily said. 'I am capable of going on this journey. And just because I am a *girl,* I am not being allowed to do what I can to help my people!'

'You're right, Lily,' Agatha said. 'Girls just don't do this sort of thing in Selsior, or in any of the Fourteen Realms, I'd guarantee. That's the way it is.'

'Well, it shouldn't be,' Lily said.

'But it is,' Agatha insisted.

Lily sighed. 'I don't want to talk about it anymore, Mum.'

'Do you want us to go?' Agatha asked.

'Yes,' Lily said coldly.

Agatha got up from the bed and gestured to Benjamin that they should leave. Benjamin shook his head as he exited the room.

'Your dad and I love you no matter what you do, Lily,' Agatha said. 'We always have and we always will. You know that, don't you?'

'I do know that, Mum,' Lily said quietly.

'And you know that you don't have to prove anything to us,' Agatha said.

'Yes, I know,' Lily said.

'Good,' Agatha said.

After Agatha had closed the door behind her, both Edwin and Hilary entered.

'What are you doing here?' Lily asked them both angrily. 'I want to be alone!'

'Do you really want to go and find this Witch in Zelnia?' Edwin asked mockingly. 'How silly. That's such a silly plan!'

'Go away, Edwin,' Lily said.

'Yes, go away, Edwin,' Hilary said too.

Laughing, Edwin ran out of the room and shut the door behind him. Meanwhile, Hilary stepped closer to Lily. Lily looked at her sister, wondering why she was still there.

'I think it sounds like you are very clever and very brave, Lily,' Hilary said. 'The cleverest and bravest person I know. I am very proud to have you as my sister. I want to be just like you when I am your age.'

With a tear in her eye, Lily brought Hilary close and hugged her. 'Thank you, Hilary,' she said, 'that means a lot to me. Especially now. And I am proud to have you as my sister too. But you shouldn't be just like me when you're my age. You should be the best that *you* can be.'

'All right,' Hilary said with a smile.

Lily smiled back at Hilary, who then ran out of the room jauntily.

The Empress of the Goblins sat in her throne, wearing her golden armour and her black jagged crown. Whatever time of the day, and whatever she was doing, the Empress always wore her armour and her crown.

The throne on which the Empress was sitting was in a room called, rather unimaginatively, the Throne Room, located at the heart of the Palace of Selsior. This was the chamber of the Palace that had been used by the Kings and Queens of Selsior to formally receive visitors and guests, and there had been two royal seats in the room for that very reason. But when the Empress took over the Palace, she ripped out one of them, so there was just one magnificent throne left for her.

The Empress was gazing at a statue of herself that had been carved by her human subjects. She had become so used to seeing these tremendous tributes to her glory and splendour as ruler of the Kingdom of Selsior that they no longer really impressed her. But the Empress now found herself admiring this particular statue because she was reminded of where she had come from. And it was this particular story that she decided to tell one of the servants in the Throne Room.

'Can I tell you a story?' the Empress asked him. It was not a question to which there really was a yes or no answer – the servant was going to hear the Empress' story whether he was interested or not.

'Um, yes, Your Imperial Majesty,' the servant said nervously.

'Good,' the Empress said with a smirk. 'You see, when I was a young Goblin princess, I was always being told where I stood in the scheme of things. As I was a female Goblin, I was not seen to be as important as the males, although I was the firstborn. So I kept myself to myself and did not ask for anything I knew I would not get.

'But as I grew older, I grew *bolder*. I wanted to have things for myself. I wanted power and control. So when the time came for my father, the Emperor of the Goblins, to divide his legacy between his spawn, he passed me over, as he did not think I had the right or the capability to govern my kind. And I was angry, I was livid, I was incandescent with rage, so... when my father died, *inexplicably*, I eliminated all of my brothers and became Empress.

'I then endeavoured to become the greatest commander of the Goblins that there had ever been. And that endeavour has culminated in the most excellent thing that the Goblins could ever dream of, and something which my father could never have even imagined: the invasion and conquest of the Kingdom of Selsior. On *my* watch and under *my* leadership.'

The servant gulped. 'The Goblins must be so happy and pleased to have you as their leader, Your Imperial Majesty,' he said.

'You are too kind,' the Empress said. 'You may resume your work now.'

And with that order, the servant went back to whatever job he had been doing.

The Empress, meanwhile, continued to look at the statue of herself, and mused on the fact that her father had never had a statue of *him* carved in stone by the people of Selsior. Neither had *he* ever taken up residence in the Palace of the Kingdom of Selsior. Oh, to be surpassed by the daughter he had never really wanted, the Empress thought to herself; he must have been turning in his Goblin grave...

Chapter 4

SETTING OFF

A week later, in the Great Hall, five boys were standing dressed in black. They stood like soldiers – backs straight, shoulders back, heads high, hands behind, looking directly ahead – in front of a small group of men from the Kingdom. The men had managed to sneak into the Great Hall for one last meeting without being seen by Goblins.

The boys had been chosen for their fitness, or their intelligence, or their toughness, or their courage, or all of those qualities combined, from among the sons of the men gathered. This had been done through a cobbled-together voting process which had taken place over the last few days.

The first was called Matthew, who was twelve-years-old, tall, well-built and tanned, with sandy blonde curly hair and blue eyes. The second was Jonathan, who was eleven-years-old, also tall, with olive skin, brown hair, hazel eyes, and with a distinct birthmark on his right cheek. The third was Timothy, who was twelve-years-old, *also tall,* with black hair, brown eyes, dark skin, and a scar above his left eyebrow. The fourth was Stephen, who was thirteen-years-old, with ginger hair, fair skin with freckles, blue eyes, sticking-out ears and quite a few spots – and he was tall as well! The fifth was Gregory, who was eleven-years-old, the shortest of the group, with hair so blonde it was almost white, pale skin, and piercing blue eyes; he was also the chubbiest of the group.

'Here are the five bravest boys of the Kingdom of Selsior!' Benjamin said proudly, to the rapturous applause of the men assembled. 'Matthew, Jonathan, Timothy, Stephen and Gregory, we are sending you on a dangerous but essential mission: to venture through, then beyond, the Forest on the northern border of Selsior, to find the Witch in the Land of Zelnia, to plead for her to come and deliver us from the tyranny of our Goblin rulers.' Benjamin could be known for his long-winded way of saying rather simple things. 'All of our hope is in the five of you now, to turn this tide in our favour. Only you can help pave the way to restoring the Kingdom of Selsior to its former glory.'

Benjamin took a step closer towards the five boys and looked at each of them intently as he spoke again: 'You know what to expect when you enter that Forest: namely Fairies, Bats, Gnomes and Giants. And watch out for any other foul creatures that might be lurking in there. I advise you not to fight any of these creatures, but to try and pass through the different parts of the Forest unseen, if you can.'

Matthew, the self-proclaimed natural leader of "the team", as he called it, was the one to ask the question on all of their minds: 'But what should we do if one of us, or some of us, are attacked by the creatures?'

Benjamin sighed, then responded: 'This is a hard thing to say, but my instruction to all of you is that if one of you is attacked, or a few of you are, those who are able *must* leave the others behind, in order to fulfil the quest. You cannot put the survival of each other above the survival of the Kingdom of Selsior. That is the harsh truth of the matter.'

'We understand, sir,' Matthew said.

'The time has come, gentlemen, for you to embark on your mission. Are you fully prepared?'

'We are,' the boys said in unison.

'Let's go then,' Benjamin said, before turning to lead the boys out.

The five boys picked up their backpacks, slung them onto their shoulders, and fell in behind Benjamin as they exited the Great Hall.

Lily was waiting outside the Great Hall as her father, the five boys, and the small group of men all came out together. She looked at the boys and was incredibly jealous of them, as they had been given the mission that she so desperately wanted to help accomplish. Was there still a way that she could be involved? Could she still go on the journey somehow? Her mind was whirring with all of the possible ways she could join the boys on the task ahead. Then she came to a decision.

Lily started running back to her house. She was running so fast that she did not notice the Goblin ahead of her – the Goblin with which she then collided.

'Oh, sorry!' Lily said. 'I'm so sorry. I didn't see you.'

The Goblin got up and put his claw beneath Lily's chin. 'Give me one reason why I shouldn't kill you right here on the spot!'

'Um, because I'm cleverer and faster than you?' Lily said, before raising her head off the Goblin's claw and running like the wind, the quickest she had ever sprinted in her whole life. The Goblin, meanwhile, lumbered after her, growling and roaring, tormented by a wound he had received in battle long ago.

Lily reached her house, went through the front door and ran straight to her bedroom. She thought about what she was going to wear, but then thought that her grey jumper and blue trousers were suitable for the journey. But she took off her black shoes and put on her brown walking boots. Instead of her grey cloak, she put on her green raincoat, which would of course be better for inclement weather conditions.

Lily got a black rucksack from one of her cupboards and placed her book in it. She got a lantern and a matchbox, as well as a notebook and a pencil, from some shelves and put those in. She then went to the kitchen and speedily made a sandwich, and got a glass bottle of water to pack in her rucksack too, as well as a few other provisions.

Lily was looking in the cupboards for any other supplies she felt she might need when she felt another person's presence in the kitchen. She span around and saw Edwin looking into her rucksack.

'What are you doing?' Edwin asked. It was a rhetorical question on Edwin's part – he knew exactly what Lily was doing.

'Shush!' Lily said. 'Be quiet.'

'I'm going to tell Mum,' he said as he bolted.

Lily followed her brother into the living room, where her mother was sitting reading. Lily could not believe that she was about to be thwarted at this point – she had plucked up the courage to take the action which she felt was necessary, only for her brother to spoil it.

'Mum,' Edwin said, 'Lily's packing her bag. I think she's going somewhere.'

Agatha put her book down and stood up. 'Lily, is this true?'

Lily sighed. 'Yes. Yes, it's true.'

'Well, where are you going?' Agatha asked.

'You know where I was planning to go...' Lily said glumly.

'Into the Forest,' Agatha said.

'I can help!' Lily exclaimed.

'We're not going to talk about this again, Lily,' Agatha said. 'I'm tired of your stubbornness. You are grounded. Go to your bedroom.'

Lily turned, dejected, and walked back to her bedroom, closing the door behind her. Agatha put her arm around Edwin.

'Thank you for telling me, Edwin,' Agatha said. 'It's for Lily's own good, but she just doesn't know it yet.'

'I hope she's not cross with me,' Edwin said sadly.

'She'll thank you one day,' Agatha said, stroking her son's hair.

The occasion was very solemn as the parents of Matthew, Jonathan, Timothy, Stephen and Gregory said their farewells to their sons. The parents embraced the boys and told them how proud they were, how the boys were so courageous, and how they were looking forward to the boys returning. Deep down though, the parents suspected they would never see their sons again. But at least they knew that their sons were lost to them for the sake of their homeland.

The boys then walked to the edge of the Forest, led by Benjamin, who was enjoying acting like the captain of a small squad of heroic soldiers. The boys turned to look at their parents one more time, possibly for the final time, then looked to Benjamin. Benjamin gave them his last few words of counsel before indicating that it was time to go into the Forest. At that moment, some Goblins patrolling the border of Selsior saw Benjamin point towards the Forest and detected trouble.

As pre-planned, the five boys ran into the Forest while the men chosen by Benjamin attacked the Goblins to stop them pursuing the boys. Matthew, Jonathan, Timothy, Stephen and Gregory all ran swiftly through the trees, not daring to look behind them. The clash between the men and the Goblins was over fairly quickly, as the men managed to prevail over their opponents with newfound ferocity. The mission on which the boys had just embarked seemed to have boosted the men's morale and inspired them. They began to believe that the Goblins could now be overcome.

The men then looked optimistically into the Forest for the first time in years, as they saw the five boys become dots in between the tree trunks. They longed for the day the boys would come back; with any luck, they would have a powerful Witch from the Land of Zelnia beside them on their return.

Lily could not believe it when she saw that her bedroom window had been nailed shut by her parents to stop her getting out again. She had to join the boys on the journey through the Forest.

The creatures could be aggressive, they could be violent, but if somebody spoke to them, if somebody said the right things, then they could be friendly and understanding. They were only aggressive and violent because they had been treated so abysmally by the Goblins for so many years. The book that Lily possessed contained all the right things to say to each kind of creatures. And Lily thought about the Witch on the other side of the Forest. How were the five boys going to ask her to help them? Did they know the right words to say to her? Did they understand the ways of the Magical Folk at all?

So what to do? Lily thought about her parents' concern for her safety – they were her parents, it was their job to be worried about that. But their concern for her was getting in the way of her helping to save the Kingdom of Selsior. She was the owner of the vitally important book, from which she had learned so much. The boys in the Forest had not been taught what they needed to know to get through it in one piece, or to successfully win over the Witch so she would help the people of Selsior.

Once again, Lily made her decision. She walked over to her rucksack, which she had left still packed in the corner of her bedroom. Very calmly, Lily picked up the rucksack and flung it as hard as she could at her bedroom window. The pane of glass shattered noisily and the shards fell to the ground outside like razor-sharp snowflakes.

Lily was convinced that the racket of the window breaking was so loud that her family must have heard. But there was no movement or sound coming from wherever in the house her parents and siblings were. Taking the opportunity, Lily climbed out of the window, lifted her rucksack onto her shoulders and set off.

Lily walked as casually as she possibly could through the roads and streets of Selsior. Her mind was buzzing with so many thoughts: *What were her parents going to do when they found out she was gone? Would she make it into the Forest without a Goblin or a whole group of Goblins seeing her? Would she catch up with the five boys in the Forest even if she did make it in there somehow?*

Every one of those questions, and many more, would remain unanswered until each of the moments arrived. All Lily knew for now was that she was about to embark upon a momentous journey, having already taken a momentous decision to escape her house after being grounded. However much guidance and wisdom she found in the pages of her book, she was still going to be venturing into the relative unknown.

And it was the unknown that Lily promptly faced: the Forest lay before her, as tall and as large as it had always been since she first saw it as a four-year-old girl. It had seemed like the stuff of nightmares then, and it was not really any less scary now. Lily looked around her, and she did not see anybody looking in her direction. So she took her chance: with one rapid movement, Lily entered the Forest and began her journey.

Twigs snapped underfoot as Lily walked through the undergrowth in the Forest. She had made it in! She had got this far without being attacked and killed by something or someone – Lily was proud of that.

Lily looked all around her at the tall, imposing trees surrounding her. Squirrels dashed up the trees, very soon out of sight. She looked further up, at the canopy, and saw a few clouds in between the tree crowns. Orange leaves dropped from branches and one leaf got caught in Lily's hair. A cool breeze glided through the Forest, and for a moment Lily was covered in leaves. She brushed them off her shoulders and walked a little further. Lily inhaled the earthy smell of the autumnal foliage around her.

All of a sudden, a swarm of flies hit Lily's face. 'Oh, go away! Go away!' Lily said as she swatted the flies. She thought she must have looked rather mad and undignified as she performed this defensive dance, with her eyes closed and her arms flailing around.

The flies eventually did go away and Lily started to run through the Forest to elude another airborne attack. The weight of the book in her rucksack prevented her from moving as fast as she could. She wished the author had written a paperback version, which would have been a tad lighter to carry.

Matthew, Jonathan, Timothy, Stephen and Gregory were sitting on some logs taking a break from the journey when they heard the sound. It was the sound of a twig breaking.

Their minds all went into a state of overdrive as they imagined Goblins attacking and capturing them, with their claws and teeth, and swords and daggers. They imagined the coldness of the dungeon walls and floor, how they would never see their parents again, and their unbearable existence in the gloominess of the Goblin dungeons.

The boys had been told by Benjamin not to confront any creatures they encountered, so they prepared to start running. But before they could get ready, they saw the face of a human girl their age pop her head round from behind a tree. Lily's eyes widened with the relief of finding the group of boys. Although she was the most knowledgeable, Lily thought it would be good to be accompanied by the group – there was an inherent safety in numbers after all.

'Lily?' Matthew exclaimed. 'What are you doing here? You shouldn't be here!'

'But here I am!' Lily said as she joined the boys. 'Shall we proceed?'

'No,' Jonathan said. 'You can't come with us. You're not supposed to come with us. Your dad said so.'

'I can help you navigate your way through this Forest unharmed,' Lily said. 'You see, there are creatures in here who just need to be spoken to in the right way and they will let you pass. Fairies, Bats, Gnomes and Giants – they are not so scary once you get to know them. And I know how to interact with them because I have read all about them–'

'Yes, in your precious book,' Timothy said dismissively. 'We are all sick and tired of hearing about this amazing book full of very interesting facts about the Forest and about the Witch.'

'It's true though – the book does contain the information necessary to make it through to the Land of Zelnia,' Lily said.

'If the book is so important, why don't you just give it to us and then you can go back to Selsior?' Stephen asked brusquely.

'That wouldn't really work,' Lily said. 'I've been reading this book for ages and I know it almost inside out. If I gave it to you, you'd have to be reading and studying it at the same time as going on the journey, which just wouldn't be practical. I don't think so anyway.'

'She does have a point,' Gregory said under his breath.

'Shut up, Gregory!' Matthew said sharply. He then turned to Lily. 'What *is* so good about this book?'

'It was written by someone who is actually an expert on the cultures of the different kinds in the Forest, and on the Witch in Zelnia,' Lily said. 'With me alongside you, you won't be knocking on the Witch's door with no idea of what to say to her!' Lily paused for a few moments, and the boys didn't talk either. 'Let me join you,' she implored. 'Let me *help* you.'

'We really should take you back,' Jonathan said. 'Your dad will be angry that we let you come with us.'

'It's too dangerous to go back now,' Lily said. 'There could be Goblins looking for you in the southern section of the Forest. We need to carry on. Together.'

'I think Lily's right, Matthew,' Timothy said.

'We should carry on,' Stephen said.

'Yes, we should carry on,' Gregory said quietly. 'That would be my vote.'

Matthew sighed, then nodded his head. 'All right, all right,' he said. 'We'll carry on through the Forest. I suppose your book might just come in useful along the way. Come on, everyone, we've been stationary for too long. Let's go.'

And with that, they set off further into the Forest. Lily hoped that she would soon be accepted as the sixth member of the group.

Chapter 5

COMPETING

Agatha walked apprehensively to Lily's bedroom door. She thought she had wisely left enough time for Lily to stew in her frustration and resentment, but felt it was now time to reconnect with her daughter.

She knocked on the door gently. 'Lily, how are you doing?' she asked.

There was no answer, so she knocked again. 'Lily?'

But there was still no answer. Agatha knew that Lily was annoyed with her but she expected some kind of response, even if it was an instruction to go away.

Agatha opened the door and entered the room. The fact that Lily was not there failed to be the first thing she noticed. The first thing she did notice, however, was the broken window. Agatha ran to the window and stuck her head outside the gap where a pane of glass had once been. She looked down and saw the shards of glass all over the ground outside.

Agatha did not know what to think, what to feel, what to do.

She admired Lily's intelligence and self-confidence; indeed, she had tried to nurture those qualities through encouraging Lily's love of reading and learning. But she could not believe that Lily had taken the extraordinary step of breaking the glass in her bedroom window, and of disobeying her parents by going into the Forest to find the Witch in the Land of Zelnia.

Agatha knew her eldest daughter could be a strong-minded and defiant girl, but she did not think Lily would go *this* far.

'Benjamin!' Agatha shrieked.

'Yes?' Benjamin said all the way from the living room.

'Come here!' Agatha demanded.

After a few moments, Benjamin joined Agatha in Lily's bedroom.

'What is it?' Benjamin asked calmly.

'Look!' Agatha replied.

'Oh, my goodness,' Benjamin said. 'What happened?'

'*Our daughter* happened...' Agatha said. 'She broke the glass in the window to make her escape.'

'You're joking?' Benjamin said.'

'No, I am not joking,' Agatha said.

'Lily's gone into the Forest?' Benjamin asked.

'It seems that way,' Agatha answered.

'Why would she do that?' Benjamin said, scratching his head.

'Because we didn't let her go,' Agatha said. 'She was determined to go on the journey to Zelnia, and so she's gone the only way she knew she could – by sneaking out.'

'But we were preventing her from going for her own good!' Benjamin said, exasperated.

'I know that! But she was obviously certain that she *had* to go,' Agatha said.

'I can't believe she would put herself in such danger after we specifically told her not to,' Benjamin said. 'I can't believe she would be so selfish...'

'She might never come back, Ben...,' Agatha said forlornly.

'She will, Agatha,' Benjamin said, desperately trying to offer solace to his wife. 'I'm sure she'll come back.'

Benjamin put his arm around Agatha and she wept on his shoulder. In his heart, Benjamin was sure that Lily would *not* be coming back, however much he wanted to persuade himself otherwise.

Lily and her five companions walked through the Forest. You might think that they would be undertaking their mission with the seriousness it deserved, but instead they were loudly arguing among themselves.

'I don't care what you say, Jonathan,' Matthew said, 'we all know that *I* am the strongest one here.'

'That's just not true!' Jonathan said.

'No, *I'm* the strongest one here,' Timothy said.

'Don't be ridiculous,' Jonathan said.

'I might actually be the strongest one here,' Stephen said coolly.

'You want to put this to the test?' Matthew asked all of them.

'Are you really doing this?' Lily asked in disbelief.

'Let's arm wrestle!' Jonathan said enthusiastically.

Jonathan ran over to a log and put his bent elbow on it with his hand open, waiting for an opponent. One by one, the boys all arm wrestled each other, with Lily reluctantly playing the part of the referee. The results of the competition are too boring yet complicated to explain, but suffice to say, Matthew ended up as the overall winner. The four other boys were irritated about their losses, but then tried to come up with other ways they could look like top dog.

It was Jonathan's idea that they should have a race. He asked Lily to pick out two trees: one from which they would start and the other which would be the finish line.

‘On your mark, get set, go,’ Lily said to begin the race. A part of Lily could not believe that she was having any role in these petty rivalries between the boys, but another part of her was pleased that they had accepted her into the group.

The boys raced from the first tree to the tree at the finishing line. Jonathan threw up his arms in the air as he crossed the finishing line before the others. Matthew was second, Stephen was third, Timothy was fourth, and Gregory was last. All of them shook their heads with disappointment at the result. Matthew was claiming that Jonathan cheated by taking off before Lily said “go”. But this claim was not treated seriously by anybody.

It was Timothy’s idea to have a tree-climbing contest, as some of the tree branches were low enough for the boys to get a foothold. So the five boys each chose a tree to climb and then began the race upwards. Stephen was the one who had chosen the most sensibly, as there were lots of branches to exploit in order to ascend ever higher. After a little while, Stephen stood victoriously on the uppermost branch in his tree, while carefully balancing himself.

'Behold the winner!' he bellowed.

'Shush!' Lily said. 'You'll draw attention to us!'

'Sorry,' Stephen said.

'All of you come down now,' Lily said. 'We should make some progress.'

The boys all descended and joined Lily on the forest floor.

'Come on, let's go,' Matthew said, trying to resume his role as the leader of the group.

They began walking further through the Forest, in silence. The boys all looked at each other, something which Lily noticed.

'What is it?' she asked, coming to a halt. The boys all stopped walking too.

'Who's the best out of the five of us?' Stephen asked.

'What do you mean?' Lily asked.

'Who's the best?' Stephen repeated. 'Out of me, Matthew, Jonathan, Timothy or Gregory? There has to be one who's the best.'

'Why? It doesn't matter who's the strongest, or the quickest, or the fastest at climbing trees,' Lily said. 'You shouldn't feel that your sense of worth comes from any of those abilities.'

'But those things are what we've always been taught are important,' Timothy said.

'Have you ever been told that you're loved and cherished just for being you?' Lily asked all of them. 'Not for what you've accomplished?'

They all shook their heads with realisation. All of their lives, the boys had been told that they had to be the fittest, the cleverest, the toughest, the bravest, the most disciplined, and better than all of the other boys in the Kingdom of Selsior. Averageness and mediocrity were not allowed. Under the Goblin occupation, their parents, as well as many other parents, had tirelessly worked to make their sons the best future soldiers for the inevitable great war with the Goblins to regain the Kingdom, rather than allow their children to just be children.

When the people of Selsior were told in secret that a plan was being developed to send a group of boys through the Forest to find the Witch in the Land of Zelnia, so many parents wanted their son to be a member of this courageous fellowship. The parents of Matthew, Jonathan, Timothy, Stephen and Gregory felt immensely proud and privileged when the boys were selected to form the group.

Lily looked at all of the boys compassionately. 'You don't have to prove your value to me, or to each other, or to anybody for that matter,' she said. 'All you have to do is do your best. And do it for yourselves, not to impress anyone else.'

The boys nodded their heads in agreement with, and appreciation of, Lily's words.

'Now come on, let's go,' Lily said. And the group started walking again.

Back in Selsior, the Goblins were even harsher towards the people because of the business on the edge of the Forest, where five of their kind were slain. Fortunately, however, the Goblins did not actually know that boys from the Kingdom had entered the Forest. But the Goblins were realising afresh that the people had some rebelliousness left in their hearts. This needed to be stamped out for good.

They put even more people in the dungeons for the smallest things, such as when a man accidentally stepped on a Goblin's foot while he was walking around the marketplace. The Goblin seethed with fury, and personally hauled the guilty man to his new residence in the Troll-guarded dungeon where he would see out the rest of his days.

More people were forced to go into the mines to extract coal in order to heat the Palace, because the Empress had been complaining that she was getting a little chilly. The Goblins wanted the Empress to be completely comfortable all of the time, so they worked their hardest to make sure that this was the case, or rather, they commanded the people of Selsior to work *their* hardest to make sure that this was the case.

And when the people were not seen to be working hard enough, the Goblins pushed them around and whacked them with truncheons. Benjamin witnessed a man being hit by one of the Goblins in the coal mine, and he wished he could tell the man that the Reign of the Goblins could be over very soon. Somewhere in the Forest, there were hopefully six children still alive, who were on their way to find the one person who could put an end to all of the people's sorrow and suffering.

Lily and the five boys had been walking for quite a while when a tired Lily turned round to the boys.

'I need a rest,' she said. 'Can we take a rest?'

'Yes,' Timothy said. 'Thank goodness, I thought I was the only one!'

'I'm very tired,' Gregory said as he sat on a log, soon followed by Lily.

Matthew led the other three boys to join Gregory and Lily on the log.

Gregory opened up his bag and pulled out a sandwich. 'I need to eat,' he said as he took a bite.

'Yes, me too,' Stephen said.

They each took their sandwiches out of their backpacks and started eating them. For a few moments, they sat eating in silence, until:

'Ugh! What's in your sandwich?' Matthew asked Gregory.

'Peanut butter and banana,' Gregory said.

'Ugh!' Jonathan, Timothy and Stephen all exclaimed.

'What's wrong with it?' Gregory asked.

'It's revolting, that's what's wrong with it,' Matthew said.

'No, it's not, it's delicious,' Gregory said. 'Well, what have you all got in your sandwiches?'

'I've got ham and cheese,' Matthew said.

'Just ham,' Stephen said.

'Chicken,' Timothy said.

'Egg,' Jonathan said lastly.

'Well, they're all original(!)' Gregory said.

'It's better to eat something unoriginal than *disgusting*,' Jonathan said.

'Are we really having this conversation?' Lily asked.

'What do you have?' Matthew asked her.

'Jam,' Lily said.

'That's fine,' Matthew said.

'Thank you for your approval,' Lily said sarcastically.

Once they had all eaten up their sandwiches, they set off again, feeling replenished. Lily and

Matthew were both towards the front of the group, like they were co-leading an expedition into the wilderness.

It was Timothy who first spotted the pond. The water was a beautiful blue and it looked very inviting.

'Let's have a swim in the pond!' Timothy suggested merrily.

'Yeah! That's a great idea!' the other boys said.

'I don't think that *is* such a great idea actually,' Lily said. 'You shouldn't get your clothes all soggy and damp. They'll take ages to dry out.'

'Oh, come on, Lily,' Matthew said. 'It'll be fun. Have some fun once in a while.'

The boys all took their top clothing off, rolled up their trousers and removed their boots, and slid into the pond. They swam around for a while, with Matthew, Jonathan, Timothy and Stephen confidently doing a front crawl, while Gregory did a doggy paddle. Soon enough, however, they had resorted to splashing each other in the face. Lily sat watching this with a mixture of amusement and mild disapproval.

'The water is so nice and warm, Lily!' Stephen said. 'Are you sure you don't want to join us?'

'Quite sure, thank you,' Lily said.

'But it's so nice,' Stephen repeated.

Out of the corner of his eye, Gregory saw a movement in the trees. He turned to look at the trees and noticed something flying from the branches to the water, and then it dived into the water.

'What was that?' Gregory asked.

'What was what?' Jonathan asked flippantly.

'Something went into the water,' Gregory said.

'We're in the middle of the Forest, Gregory, there are going to be lots of "somethings" around,' Jonathan said.

'Ow!' Timothy yelled suddenly.

Lily stood up. 'What is it?' she asked.

'Something in the water just hurt me,' Timothy said. 'Ow!' he yelled again.

'What is it?' Matthew asked.

'I don't know!' Timothy cried. 'I don't know what it is!'

What it was soon revealed itself: a Fairy rose out of the water and prodded Timothy on the forehead. And before they knew it, the boys were surrounded by Fairies, some of whom gathered together so they had the strength to lift a couple of the boys out of the water, fly over to the Forest floor and drop them, and not as delicately as you might imagine.

'Ouch,' Jonathan said as he landed with a bump on the muddy ground.

Stephen soon joined him. 'Ouch,' he said too, as he rubbed his sore bottom.

'Fairies!' Lily said elatedly.

Matthew, Timothy and Gregory all got out of the water and scrambled to get their tops and boots back on.

'We need to get away from here!' Matthew said, terrified. 'They're going to kill us. They're going to kill us!'

'Calm down, Matthew,' Lily said reassuringly. 'It's all right.'

'How do you know that?' Jonathan asked. 'Did you see how strong they are? They just lifted me and Stephen out of the water and dumped us here! They could kill us.'

'They won't if we just explain ourselves,' Lily said.

'What are you going to "explain" to them exactly?' Matthew asked.

'I will explain to them what they want to know,' Lily said.

Lily then turned to the Fairies, who were now completely encircling the group. The Fairies looked very much like human women, but of course a lot smaller, being just one foot tall or so; they were wearing different colour dresses: blue, white, purple, pink, and yellow; and possessed elegant wings which resembled those of a butterfly.

One of the Fairies, wearing a silver dress and with a glittering tiara upon her head, presented herself to Lily, who seemed to the Fairy to be the obvious leader of the group. Lily knew that this was the Queen of the Fairies.

The Fairies were the last kind of creatures to make their home in the Forest between Selsior and Zelnia. They had lived in the Ancient Woodland in the West, alongside the Magical Folk. The Wizards and Witches helped them set up their community among the pine trees, and they lived in peace and harmony for thousands of years. But when the Magical Folk decided to leave to live in the Land of Zelnia, the Fairies wanted to follow the magic, so they made their new home in the Forest, but they found that they were not alone.

'Who are you and what are you doing in the realm of the Fairies of the Forest?' the Queen of the Fairies asked curtly.

'O beautiful and magnificent Queen of the Fairies,' Lily answered confidently, as well as a bit exaggeratedly, 'we are children from the Kingdom of Selsior. My name is Lily, and their names are Matthew, Jonathan, Timothy, Stephen, and Gregory.' As she said each name, Lily pointed at the boy belonging to it. 'And we are on a journey through the Forest to the Land of Zelnia beyond, to find the Witch there. We are going to ask her to come and get rid of the Goblins, who, as I'm sure you know, invaded and conquered Selsior twelve years ago.'

'Ah, I see,' the Queen of the Fairies said. 'But why have the people of Selsior sent children instead of grown-ups?'

'Magical Folk tend to respond to children more because of their innocence and their open-mindedness to magic,' Lily replied, 'as is evident, I hope, in our response to you and your kind, Your Highness. We have not retaliated, even though you took hold of two of my friends here and moved them without asking their permission first! Instead, we are merely admiring how lovely you all look and how quiet and peaceful your realm is. Your Highness, we only seek to pass through your realm to continue on our journey. Please do not delay us any longer.'

The Queen of the Fairies looked closer at Lily. 'I can see in your eyes that your intentions are noble and pure,' she said. 'And I am very pleased with the sound of your task, for the Goblins were very cruel to us when they ruled the Forest, due to our size. They thought they could boss us around and treat us like little playthings.'

'The Goblins have been cruel to the people of Selsior ever since they took over the Kingdom,' Lily said. 'They have pushed us around and hit us, for no reason at all; they have imprisoned people, just because they can. I suppose we have our mistreatment by the Goblins in common with each other. And we want to put an end to it, once and for all.'

'And you think the Witch you seek will help you with this?' the Queen of the Fairies asked. 'Regrettably, we have not seen any of the Magical Folk in many, many years. They used to wander through the Forest so often. But they do not pass through here anymore.'

'We hope that the Witch will want to help us, yes,' Lily said. 'The Magical Folk rescued the Kingdom of Selsior from the Goblins once before. When the Witch hears about our plight, I am certain she will rescue the Kingdom again.'

'Well, we will allow you to pass, Lily of Selsior,' the Queen of the Fairies said, 'along with your companions, because you have been respectful to us. You have not looked at us as if we are insignificant, or lesser than you. And we thank you for your respect. It is a rare thing in this Forest. You go now with our blessing.'

'Thank you, Your Highness,' Lily said.

'We are sorry for how we made our presence known to you,' the Queen of the Fairies said, 'and for how we removed you from the pond. You may resume your swimming, if you like!'

'Apology accepted, Your Highness!' Lily said.

'I hope the other creatures of the Forest will be as courteous to you as we have been,' the Queen of the Fairies said. 'I would not count on it.'

The Queen of the Fairies then flew away and the rest of the Fairies soon followed her. Lily did not see where they went. It was like they just vanished! When Lily turned around, Matthew was picking up his bag.

'I'm not doing this anymore,' he said. 'I'm not going any further.'

'What do you mean?' Jonathan asked.

'I'm not going any further!' Matthew restated. 'I'm scared of this Forest and I want to go home.'

'But you're our leader,' Stephen said. 'You're supposed to be the bravest out of all of us. Why are you leaving us?'

'I didn't really think that there would be creatures in here,' Matthew said. 'I thought they were just stories, myths, fairy tales, if you'll pardon the pun... I don't want to meet the Bats, the Gnomes, and the Giants. One of them is going to kill us. I know it. Now you can do what you want, but I'm going home.' And with that, Matthew set off running back towards Selsior.

'Matthew!' Jonathan shouted. 'You can't leave us now!'

'You should lower your voice, Jonathan,' Lily said. 'So not to bother any more creatures of the Forest...'

Lily and the four remaining boys watched in shock as Matthew soon disappeared from sight. The boy who was supposed to be the bravest and the toughest of the group had given up on the mission and was gone.

Chapter 6

WINGS

'I can't believe Matthew is scared of *Fairies*!' Jonathan said with derision in his voice.

Lily was silent as she led Jonathan, Timothy, Stephen and Gregory further into the Forest. She too could not really believe that Matthew had abandoned them so soon into the journey, but she was not going to join in with the four boys teasing him.

'Yes, what a scaredy-cat!' Stephen said. 'Those Fairies were harmless.'

'They did pick you up and dump you on the ground though!' Timothy said.

'I let them! I thought it was fun,' Stephen said defensively. 'But I wasn't going to run back home because of them!'

‘What did Matthew think they were going to do? Sprinkle fairy dust in his eyes and blind him?’ Jonathan asked mockingly.

‘Look, can you stop poking fun at Matthew?’ Lily asked. ‘Everybody gets scared at one time or another. Matthew obviously feared what he was going to come across in the Forest and felt he couldn’t persevere. That is his business, not any of ours. None of us can judge him.’

The boys all fell silent after Lily had said this. They were prone to ridiculing others when they showed weakness or failure of any kind, as a way to make them feel better about themselves. But they knew that Lily was right – a time would come when fear would overcome them. They worried about the creatures they might encounter in the Forest, and whether Lily would be able to charm all of them enough that they would let the group pass.

Lily could see that the boys were now looking downhearted. She turned to them. ‘Are you all right?’ Lily asked.

'If Matthew was the bravest of all of us,' Jonathan began, 'what chance do *we* have of making it through the Forest?'

Lily put her hand on Jonathan's shoulder, then Gregory's. 'Don't compare yourself to Matthew, or to anyone,' she said. 'Simply be the bravest that *you* can be, and that will be good enough. All right?'

The four boys all nodded, once again helped by Lily's thoughtful advice to them. The boys walked more self-assuredly now. Lily smiled as she saw their rekindled confidence clearly on their faces.

The day began to darken and the Moon intermittently peeked out from behind some clouds. Owls hooted and strange other noises could be heard in the darkness of the Forest. Night was falling, and Lily realised that there was no point in continuing, as the group could not see anything. The group came to a clearing and Lily ceased walking.

'We should stop here for the night and try to get some sleep,' Lily said.

'Yes, I think you're right,' Jonathan said. 'Who knows what we could be stepping in if we carry on in the blackness?'

'What do you mean, like puddles?' Gregory asked naïvely.

'No, I kind of mean *poo*,' Jonathan said, bursting into laughter. He was soon joined by Timothy and Stephen, who both guffawed wildly.

'It's not *that* funny,' Gregory said.

'Yes, I agree,' Lily said.

'We need some humour on this journey,' Jonathan said, 'to lighten the mood. This whole thing is very serious and dangerous.'

'Yes, I agree,' Lily said, 'as long as it's not at somebody's expense.'

'All right,' Jonathan said.

'Anyway. Let's settle down for the night,' Lily said.

The four boys each got blankets out of their backpacks. Lily looked at this and realised she had not got anything to sleep upon! This had slipped her mind. Lily was wondering about what she would do when Gregory noticed that Lily did not have a blanket.

'You can have one of mine,' he said.

'Really?' Lily asked.

'Yes, my mum packed two for me,' Gregory replied. 'One to sleep on and the other to cover myself with. But this blanket is so big that I can just wrap it around myself like a cocoon.'

'That's very kind of you, Gregory,' Lily said. 'Thank you.'

Gregory gave the blanket to Lily and she laid it down on the ground. Lily lay down on the blanket, and arranged her raincoat to cover her and keep her warm. She felt reasonably warm as she looked up at the sky full of stars.

Apart from a few clouds here and there, it was a clear night. The hooting of the owls continued, and Lily feared that the sound would prevent her from getting any sleep. She soon found that she might not get any sleep for another reason: Timothy was feeling thoughtful and reflective beneath the tree canopy, while he gazed at the twinkling stars.

'Do you think Selsior has a future?' he asked.

'What do you mean?' Lily asked.

'I mean, is there any hope for the Kingdom?' Timothy said. 'The Goblins have been ruling it for so long, is there a way it can go back to how it was, before the Goblins?'

'Selsior was a great and prosperous kingdom for hundreds of years before the Goblins took over,' Lily said. 'The rule of the Goblins will be just a short blip in its history.'

'How can you be sure?' This question came from Stephen.

'When you've read as much history as I have, you realise that The World is full of places that experience hardship, but they survive them in the end,' Lily said. 'If something is worth fighting for, it will endure one way or another.'

'You're very wise for your age, Lily,' Gregory said.

'Thank you, Gregory,' Lily said.

'Do you think that the King and Queen are still alive?' Jonathan asked. 'My parents told me that they were put into a dungeon guarded by big, fat Trolls. And the Prince is in there with them too.'

'Yes, I believe they are alive,' Lily said.

'How can you know that?' Jonathan asked.

'I just have a feeling,' Lily answered. 'A gut instinct.'

'Do you think they will ever be freed?' Stephen asked.

'Well, that's what I'm hoping the Witch is going to do,' Lily said. 'She will come and help us defeat the Goblins, and then she will release the King and Queen, and the Prince, from their imprisonment. Well, that's the plan at least.'

'Will the Witch be able to defeat the Goblins on her own?' Gregory asked. 'There are loads and loads of Goblins, but only one of her!'

'But you're forgetting the Witch has magical powers!' Lily exclaimed reassuringly. 'Magic courses through her veins, Gregory. Plus she is *good*, and good will always ultimately triumph over evil. It's just the way it goes.'

'I hope you are right,' Gregory said. 'You do seem to be right a lot of the time.'

'I try my best!' Lily said modestly, blushing at the compliment paid to her. She often got embarrassed when she was praised, even by her family.

Lily now thought of her family back in Selsior, who would be distraught at her leaving to go into the Forest. Lily was sorry to have gone without her parents' permission, or even knowledge, but desperate times call for desperate measures, she reasoned, so it had to be this way.

Lily knew that her father would be trying to keep her mother calm, but would be worrying about Lily's fate himself. She knew her brother Edwin would be acting as if nothing had happened, while playing games and making mischief as he usually did. And lastly she knew her little sister Hilary would be secretly proud of her, believing that Lily was right to go off and rescue the Kingdom, like one of the bedtime stories her mother used to read to her. Lily now began to miss her family and her home, but she knew that she had to push those feelings away, out of her mind, so she could focus on the here and now.

'Do you think *we* will survive the night?' Timothy asked, only half joking. The Forest had now gone eerily quiet, and he did not know if that was a good thing or a bad thing.

'Yes, we'll survive the night,' Lily said. 'Or at least *some* of us will. Mwahahaha!'

'That's not funny, Lily!' Jonathan said.

'You were the one who said we needed humour to lighten the mood!' Lily said. 'So I'm lightening the mood!'

'Maybe you could lighten the Forest instead,' Jonathan said. 'It's so spooky in here...'

'Let's just try to get some sleep, shall we?' Lily said. 'We'll drift off soon enough. If you all stop talking, that is.'

'Hey!' Timothy said. 'We were having a nice discussion, weren't we?'

'Yes, we were,' Lily said. 'Goodnight, everyone.'

'Goodnight, Lily,' each of the four boys said.

They did all drop off to sleep after a little while. And they each had dreams. Lily dreamt of her home and her family, of sitting beside the fireplace on a cold winter's evening, of delicious dinners and lovely cups of tea, and of sitting by her bookshelves, picking a book to read. Jonathan dreamt that he freed the King and Queen of Selsior from the Goblin dungeon; Timothy dreamt of fighting a Goblin and overcoming it; Stephen dreamt of being made a knight of Selsior; Gregory dreamt of meeting the Witch in the Land of Zelnia while he stood alongside Lily – he and Lily were the best of friends in his dream.

All of their dreams were interrupted by the sound of wings flapping. It was a terrifying noise, loud and threatening. Lily was the first to wake up, and it sounded like, and felt like, wings were flapping right by her head.

The fluttering was soon accompanied by the clap of thunder. *Oh, very helpful*, Lily thought, as rain started to come down. But what *was* helpful was that lightning soon came and it brightened her surroundings. The shadows of wings danced across the tree trunks. Lily realised what these nocturnal creatures were: Bats. The Bats were whirling overhead.

Timothy, Stephen and Gregory woke up and heard the sound of the Bats flying around them and felt the rain fall on their heads. At first, they did not know whether this was a nightmare or they had woken up and this was real life.

'Lily, what's happening?' Stephen asked in terror.

'Just remain calm,' Lily said. 'It's nothing to worry about.'

Lily opened up her rucksack and got out the lantern and the matchbox. She struck the match and she soon lit the candle inside the lantern, which helped to illuminate the area.

Jonathan was the last to wake up. He looked around at the Bats flying around them and panicked.

'Run!' Jonathan shouted. 'Everybody run!'

Jonathan sprinted off, followed by Timothy, Stephen and Gregory. The Bats swooped down and pursued the running boys. Lily ran behind the Bats and the four boys, carrying her lantern by its handle, annoyed by the fact that her companions had decided to run. The boys looked behind them, terrified, as the Bats continued to pursue them. The Bats beat their wings in an intimidating manner.

The Bats chased the boys for a while, with Lily still running behind. Lily saw a different Bat fly in front of the boys and land on the Forest floor, causing the boys to stop suddenly in their tracks. In response to this, the Bats all hung upside down from the tree branches, looking at the boys, assessing them.

Lily caught up with the boys and looked all around her at the Bats in the trees. She saw that they had very dark grey skin, blue eyes, large pointed ears, and sharp teeth, much like the bats that we are used to in our world. The Bats stretched out their arms, and the human group saw how wide their wingspans were.

The Bat standing on the Forest floor walked towards Lily and the boys. Lily noticed that this Bat was the tallest in the colony – it was five foot tall on its hind legs. It looked rather frightening, although this Bat had seemed to stop his fellow Bats chasing the boys. It looked at the group of children inquisitively. It had not seen humans in hundreds of years, and human children were certainly the last things he expected to see in the Forest, especially at this very late hour.

'So,' the Bat began, 'who exactly are you and what are you doing here in the Forest?'

Lily stepped forward, holding her lantern aloft. 'We are children from Selsior,' she said. 'My name is Lily and they are Jonathan, Timothy, Stephen and Gregory. We are on a journey through the Forest to the Land of Zelnia, to look for the Witch there, in order to ask for her help against the Goblins who have conquered our homeland. We ask that we may sleep in your territory tonight, then have a safe passage out of your part of the Forest in the morning.'

'Well, good evening, children,' the Bat said, very politely. 'I am the Master of the Bats. I am glad to make your acquaintance.'

'Good evening, Sir,' Lily responded.

'I was wondering when this day would come,' the Master of the Bats said. 'And it has come at long last. We have our own history with the Goblins. You see, hundreds of years ago, the Bats dwelt in the caves in the south. Bats yearn for the darkness, and caves are the deepest, darkest places to be found in The World.

'But when the land was carved up into the Fourteen Realms, and the Kingdom of Tinon was created in the southernmost part of the landmass, the caves there were destroyed, demolished, in the construction of a tunnel through the mountains. So the Bats needed to move elsewhere, and after quite a bit of searching, we found the Forest between the Kingdom of Selsior and the Land of Zelnia. And this is where we made our home, in roosts within the trees.

'We lived in peace for many years, alongside the other creatures; they made us feel very welcome indeed. But then the Goblins came. They took over the whole Forest and oppressed all of the creatures ruthlessly. They soon became the unopposed rulers of the Forest. And the Goblins were very jealous of our wings and of our ability to fly. So they would capture us, and some held us down while others bound our wings with ropes to prevent us from flying any longer.'

'Oh, my goodness,' Lily said. 'That's appalling! How spiteful and cruel. Well, I am so glad that the Bats of the Forest are able to take flight once again. Even if you did use them to chase my friends here!'

'Thank you very much for your kind words, Lily,' the Master of the Bats said. 'And I look forward to the people of Selsior being free of the Goblins one day soon, like the Bats are free of them now.'

'We thank you very much for *your* kind words, Sir,' Lily said.

'You may sleep here for the night now,' the Master of the Bats said. 'I am sorry that you were frightened and chased by my kin. I am sure they just wanted to know who you were and why you were in our territory! I hope you will forgive us.'

'Oh, I'm sure we can forgive you,' Lily said. 'But could we ask one favour of you, Sir?'

'Yes, of course,' the Master of the Bats replied.

'Could you and your fellow Bats please fly us back to where we were sleeping?' Lily asked. 'All of our stuff is there, and we'd appreciate it if you could help us return. I fear that we are lost now because we have run so far from where we were.'

'Yes, of course we will happily oblige,' the Master of the Bats said. 'Come down from the trees, Bats, so we can fly the children back.'

Four Bats flew down from the trees. Jonathan, Timothy, Stephen and Gregory got on those Bats' backs, while Lily got on the Master's back. Jonathan was the most reluctant – he could not believe that they were doing this, when not that long ago these same Bats were chasing him and the other boys.

The Bats zoomed off together, flying through the tree trunks at top velocity. The rain had now stopped, and the Moon glowed brightly, lighting up the sky above the Forest; there was no need for the lantern which Lily was still holding on to tightly.

Lily found the flight absolutely exhilarating – she had never travelled so quickly before! She felt the wind blow upon her face and through her hair. She held onto the Master's shoulders to cope with the sheer speed of the flight, and to steady herself as the Master sometimes flew sideways between the trees.

Timothy, Stephen and Gregory all enjoyed their flights too, as it was one of the greatest thrills they had experienced in their entire lives! Jonathan, on the other hand, was not having fun. He wanted the flight to come to an end very soon; in fact, he wanted *the whole thing* to be over very soon.

Before too long, the Bats landed where Lily and the boys had lain down for the night. The Bats extended their wings to the ground, and the children disembarked from the Bats' backs.

'Here you all are,' the Master of the Bats said. 'Have a good rest, and I hope your journey onwards is a safe and productive one.'

'Thank you, Sir,' Lily said.

The Master of the Bats took his leave and flew upwards, leading the colony of Bats to the canopy above.

Jonathan walked purposefully back to his blanket on the Forest floor. He started folding the blanket up, which Lily noticed.

'Jonathan, what are you doing?' she asked.

'I want to go home,' Jonathan said. 'I cannot bear to spend another minute in this Forest. Those Bats were chasing us earlier, hunting us! They could have caught us and killed us! Now I know that they were friendly once their Master or whoever arrived, but who knows what the next creatures will do? What if they're not so friendly? Ever?'

'We will be safe as long as we talk rationally and calmly to the creatures,' Lily said.

'Yes, using your amazing book!' Jonathan said sarcastically. 'You've had all the answers *so far* because you've read that book. But what if the book doesn't have all the answers? What if something happens to you and we're left alone with these creatures? What then?'

'Jonathan...' Lily began.

'I'm going,' he said. 'I'm leaving now.'

Jonathan shoved the blanket in his backpack, which he then buttoned up. He slung the backpack on and walked off in the direction of Selsior. Jonathan's walk soon turned into a jog. His path through the Forest was lit only by the retreating moonlight.

'Anybody else want to go while they have the chance?' Timothy asked gruffly.

Stephen and Gregory shook their heads. Lily did not feel the need to do the same, as she did not think the question was addressed to her anyway.

'Good,' Timothy said.

Lily blew out the candle in her lantern and put the lantern back in her rucksack. She and the boys then silently lay back down on their blankets, and drifted off to sleep once again. The group's first day in the Forest had well and truly come to an end.

The group from Selsior had so far encountered two kinds of creatures – the Fairies and the Bats – both of which had let them pass through their parts of the Forest. Would the same be the case when Lily, Timothy, Stephen and Gregory met the other creatures of the Forest the next day? But they were not worried about that for the moment – they rested their bodies and resumed their dreams.

Meanwhile, many miles away, Benjamin and Agatha were getting ready to go to bed. It had been an exhausting day once again for Benjamin working in the coal mine, as well as worrying about Lily in the Forest. Agatha simply did not know what to do with herself. She tried her best to go about her life as usual, but she was so concerned about her daughter that she found it difficult to function.

Dinner that evening had been strange, with Benjamin and Agatha eating with just two of their children. They had sat and eaten in silence, as none of them could muster the energy to strike up a conversation about something.

Then after dinner, the members of the family had gone off to different rooms in the house to do their own separate things: Benjamin replaced the pane of glass in Lily's bedroom window, Agatha was doing some cleaning and dusting, Edwin played with his toys, and Hilary played a few tunes on her flute.

Later, Benjamin and Agatha went to Edwin's bedroom, then Hilary's, to bid them goodnight. They walked to Lily's bedroom – they looked inside and stared at its emptiness, then closed the door behind them, as Agatha tried to hold back tears.

In the Palace of the Empress of the Goblins, the Goblins brought their leader news that they had captured a boy who had run out of the Forest.

'How had the boy got into the Forest in the first place?' the Empress asked angrily.

'We do not know, Your Imperial Majesty,' the Goblin messengers said. 'But we think it had something to do with the time our patrollers on the border of the Forest were attacked and killed.'

'Double the number of patrollers on the border of the Forest to make sure there is no more funny business,' the Empress ordered. 'I assure you that heads will roll if it is discovered that any more have entered the Forest...'

In a dungeon, a tall blonde boy was shackled to the wall. He whimpered and coughed quietly into the sleeves of his black top, which were still a bit damp from the pond he had swum around in.

Matthew decided he might have made a mistake by running back towards Selsior. When he left his companions in the Forest, he imagined that he would be returning to his family, his three meals a day, and his bed. He never even thought that he would have to watch out for Goblins on the northern border of Selsior. But he was worried more about how disappointed his parents would be in his departure from the Forest than about his survival in the Goblin dungeon.

The Troll guards had walked past a couple of times since he arrived and they had startled him. He had heard about them from stories he was read as a child and they looked exactly how he remembered: very tall and fat, with grey lumpish skin and wearing green shorts. Their clubs dragged along the ground as they walked up and down the corridor.

The cell door creaked open, and Matthew froze with fear of who or what was going to enter. The Troll ducked under the doorway carrying a plate. It walked over to the wall to which Matthew was shackled and put the plate down beside him. It had some mouldy bread on it.

'Eat,' the Troll said grumpily, before turning around and walking out of the cell. The door was slammed shut and locked.

Matthew heard the sound of keys jangling get quieter and quieter as the Troll walked away.

Chapter 7

BENEATH

It was both the sun in her eyes and the sound of birdsong that woke Lily up. She looked all around her and the Forest was bright and still. She glimpsed a clear blue sky above the canopy, and the sun shone through the branches of the trees like javelins of light. Lily could see a large spider's web between two branches glistening with dew – she wondered if the spider was finding it irksome that its home was now wet, after all the work it had gone to spinning it.

The birds were chirping at full volume, constantly changing notes like an orchestra playing a symphony. Lily had read about the different songbirds of the Forest: nightingales, blackbirds, chaffinches and cuckoos. Lily did not know which one of those was the source of this morning's musical composition – maybe it was all of them!

Even though this was obviously a very dangerous mission and an arduous journey, Lily thought one of the upsides of the whole thing was that she was finally able to be out and about in nature, and experience it in all its splendour. She had wanted to travel around and explore The World ever since she was very little. And she finally had the chance now, despite the challenging circumstances.

Lily pushed her raincoat off her and put it to one side. She stood up and stretched out her arms and yawned, despite feeling well-rested and refreshed. While doing so, she accidentally stood on a twig and it snapped loudly. Timothy, Stephen and Gregory all woke up at the sound and saw Lily standing, looking at the broken twig on the ground.

'Sorry to wake all of you!' she said.

'It was time we all got up anyway,' Timothy said. 'It's a lovely morning. Very sunny.'

'Yes, it is,' Lily said, 'certainly after all the rain and thunder and lightning last night. It has cleared and brightened up very nicely.'

'We sound like our parents,' Stephen chimed in, 'talking about the weather and whatnot.'

'But the weather is important,' Lily said, 'the sunlight will make our journey far easier.'

'Was the blanket comfortable?' Gregory asked Lily, changing the subject completely.

'Oh, yes, it was,' Lily said. 'Thank you so much, Gregory.'

'I'll pack it away in my backpack,' he said.

'All right. Thank you again,' Lily said.

'No problem,' Gregory said. 'I mean, you're welcome!'

Gregory folded up the blanket and stuffed it in his backpack, along with his own. He got out a banana and peeled the skin off, then he took a bite.

'Breakfast?' Lily asked.

'Uh-huh,' he replied, with a mouthful of banana.

'Do you have breakfast?' Lily asked Timothy and Stephen.

They both nodded and got their breakfast out of their backpacks. Timothy had an apple to munch on, while Stephen got out a raw carrot. Lily looked into her rucksack for something that she could have for breakfast. When it was obvious that she did not have anything, Timothy got out another apple and offered it to her.

'There you are,' Timothy said.

'Thank you, Timothy,' Lily said.

'Well, we can't have our group leader walking on an empty stomach, can we?' he said with a smile.

'That's very kind of you,' she said. Now Lily had known that the boys were relying on her to lead the way, and to talk to the creatures of the Forest, but for Timothy to actually go as far as calling her the group leader! It was a huge shift from when she had first joined the walking party. They were putting all of their faith and trust in her now.

The four of them finished their breakfast and set off, embarking on their second day in the Forest. They walked in silence for quite a while, each of them thinking about what they might meet on this next leg of the journey.

'What I don't really get,' Stephen said, 'is how you always know what to say to the creatures, Lily.'

'I've only absorbed the information to be found in the pages of my book,' Lily said. 'The author of my book spent years wandering around The World with a walking stick that made him invisible. And he studied the different communities and cultures that he encountered, writing it all down. He only wrote one copy of this particular book and it remained unsold for many years until I was walking through the marketplace and bought it.'

'Why didn't anybody else want to buy it?' Stephen asked.

'That I don't really know, Stephen,' Lily replied. 'Perhaps because they were not interested in reading about the places around them, when their homeland had been taken away from them... which is understandable. Also, I imagine they didn't see any point in looking back at the glorious past of Selsior, when the present was so miserable, and they didn't hold much hope for the future either.'

'I did not hold much hope for my future,' Gregory said wistfully. 'Until now, that is. We're going to make it through this Forest, find the Witch and rescue the Kingdom of Selsior!'

'That's the spirit!' Timothy said.

'Yes, I could not have said it better myself,' Lily said.

'Lead on, Lily!' Stephen said.

'Let's go!' Lily said.

Lily surged forward, like she was leading an army into battle, and the boys followed closely behind her. They seemed to have a renewed sense of purpose as they ventured ever further through the Forest. The sun continued to stream through the gaps between the branches and the birds sang their delightful melody, which was carried along on the gentle westerly breeze.

'I want a walking stick!' Timothy suddenly declared. 'I've been thinking about that author you mentioned earlier, with the walking stick that made him invisible. Well, I want to have a walking stick!'

'You do know that it wouldn't make you invisible even if you had one?' Lily said. 'The walking stick that the author had was magic – it had a spell upon it.'

'Yes, of course I know that,' Timothy said. 'But I want one nevertheless.'

Timothy ran towards one of the trees and went about trying to rip off one of its branches. He tried to get some leverage by raising his leg so his foot was flat against the trunk, and he pulled the branch as hard as he possibly could.

'You really shouldn't do that,' Lily said.

'I've nearly got it!' Timothy said, red in the face from the exertion. 'Wait one second! Just wait... one... second!'

He finally severed the branch from the tree, which caused the tree and the ground beneath them to reverberate slightly. Lily anxiously looked down, then around to see what happened as a result.

'What are you looking worried for?' Timothy asked Lily.

'You might have awakened the creatures in this part of the Forest,' Lily said.

Timothy looked around him and into the distance. 'But there obviously aren't any creatures here,' he said. 'Can you see any?'

'That's because they usually hide themselves, Timothy,' Lily said. 'Until they are *disturbed*.'

As soon as Lily had finished her sentence, the group heard the sound of rumbling beneath their feet. They looked at each other frantically, wondering whether running would help them or cause them even more of a problem.

'What's happening?' Timothy asked.

'They have come to tell us that they have been disturbed,' Lily answered. She suppressed the desire to tell him "I told you so", however tempting it was.

'Who have been disturbed?' Gregory asked.

'Gnomes!' Lily shouted.

Soon enough, a whole army of Gnomes were coming out of holes they had made in the trees to enter and exit their underground domain. The Gnomes had dwelt underneath the Forest for thousands of years, although they did come up to the surface occasionally to get some fresh air and to feel the sun on their faces. They were short, as you might expect; they looked like elderly men with hair and beards as white as snow; and they wore green jumpers, blue trousers, black belts with silver buckles around their middle, brown gloves, black boots, and red pointed hats.

There were so many Gnomes now that Lily had lost count. They seized Lily, Timothy, Stephen and Gregory and tied them all to a tree, kicking and screaming the whole time, as you might imagine! This was the first sense of real danger the children had experienced since their entry into the Forest. Even Lily was wondering how they were going to wriggle their way out of this. The Gnomes had been so quick to take hold of them and strap them to the tree trunk, that Lily had not had the opportunity to speak to them and explain why they were there.

A Gnome came up to the children. 'You will wait here until the King arrives,' he said.

'We can't exactly go anywhere, can we?' Lily remarked.

'Watch your tongue, miss,' the Gnome said. 'You will be polite to us when you are on our turf. Or *above* our turf, I should say.' He then walked away.

'We really don't mean you any harm!' Lily said, calling after the Gnome.

'Be silent while you wait for the King!' the Gnome instructed as he turned around.

Out of nowhere, some Gnomes did a short tune on their trumpets. 'His Majesty the King of the Gnomes of the Forest is here!' the heralds proclaimed, as the King was carried towards Lily and the boys on his wooden throne upon a litter. The litter was set down on the floor and the King of the Gnomes stood up and walked over to the bound children.

'Well done for capturing these trouble-making children and stopping them in their tracks,' the King of the Gnomes said proudly.

'We are not making any trouble, Your Majesty...' Lily began.

'Silence!' the King interrupted. 'You will all be sacrificed to the Goblins' Wolves who are searching the Forest. Or perhaps the Wolves could take you to their masters, who I am sure would like to know that you are here in the Forest...' He turned to the Gnomes around him: 'Send the signal for the Wolves to come here and claim their prize.'

Timothy, Stephen and Gregory all looked at each other, squirming, completely terrified. Wolves? What wolves was the King of the Gnomes referring to? They did not like the sound of any wolves being called. And the King of the Gnomes obviously meant the children when he said these wolves could "claim their prize" – who or what else would he have been talking about? Even Lily had not remembered reading about any *wolves* in the Forest... They must be *new*, she thought.

'No, no, wait!' Lily said. 'I want to explain why we're here. If you would please let me.'

'Hmm,' the King of the Gnomes said. 'Oh, go on then, if you really want to. Who are you and what are you doing here?'

'We are children from the Kingdom of Selsior – I am Lily and the boys sitting here beside me are Timothy, Stephen and Gregory. We are on a journey through the Forest to the Land of Zelnia beyond, to ask the Witch there to help the people of Selsior overthrow the Goblins and take back our homeland. Allow us to succeed in our task and the Gnomes will not have to do the Goblins' bidding any longer.'

'Oh, I see,' the King of the Gnomes said. 'But the Gnomes have a very good working relationship with the Goblins, which is mutually beneficial. So we do not need any Witch to overthrow the Goblins. That outcome would not suit *us* as much as it would obviously suit *your people*. So I must deny your request.'

'How did the Goblins get you to work for them, may I ask?' Lily inquired.

'In the past, Gnomes have been seen as inferior due to our appearance and stature, and we have been mocked and insulted because of the way we look,' the King of the Gnomes said. 'The Goblins said that working for them would help us to prosper, and to live good and rich lives. And they kept their promise: they shared many of the jewels and precious metals that they inherited when they conquered the Kingdom of Selsior. In return, we would spy for the Goblins, and inform them if and when we found any of their foes in the Forest. You will find it is... an advantageous arrangement.'

'You don't have to be the Goblins' spies anymore,' Lily said. 'You have got your gold and your precious metals; you have got a nice home here beneath the Forest. Don't you want freedom from the Goblins, not to be their minions anymore? Don't you want to be completely and totally independent of them? Let us pass and we will make sure the

Goblins are vanquished once and for all, so none of us has to live under their yoke. The people of Selsior simply want what you have now: a place to call their own again, a homeland.'

'You speak with great passion,' the King of the Gnomes said. 'You are very mature for your youth.'

'Just don't call for the Goblins' Wolves to come, and let us make progress through the Forest,' Lily said. 'That's all we ask. Nothing more.'

The King of the Gnomes sighed deeply. He remembered the time, many years ago, before the Goblins invaded and conquered the Forest. The Gnomes had lived reasonably good lives, keeping themselves to themselves, and they lived in peace. But then the Goblins arrived and they used to taunt and tease the Gnomes whenever they came across them. The King of the Gnomes had not told Lily that it was the Goblins who had originally mocked them. But he knew it was in their nature to do so – it was how they entertained themselves. So he could sympathise with the plight of the people of Selsior, especially now that he was face-to-face with these four children.

'Hmm,' the King of the Gnomes said. 'I am inclined to take pity on you and your people,' he said.

'What are you talking about?' one of the Gnomes standing behind the King said. 'You can't let them go! We must call for the Wolves and hand the children over to the Goblins, as the deal dictates.'

'Silence!' the King of the Gnomes commanded. The Gnome who had questioned the King slunk to the back of the group to hide – he did not wish to incur His Majesty's wrath. 'I will let you pass, children of Selsior, to continue on your journey. Perhaps the Goblins have been running things for far too long. Free the Kingdom of Selsior and you can free us in the process.'

'Your Majesty, we highly recommend that you change your mind,' one of the King's advisors said.

'My mind will not change,' the King of the Gnomes said. 'It will happen as I say. Untie them, and let them go.'

Some Gnomes walked towards Lily and the three boys with knives and cut the rope tying them all to the tree. The children all stood up and stretched out their arms and kicked out their legs, wanting to get some feeling back in their limbs.

The Gnomes then jumped back through the holes in the trees, returning to their home beneath the ground. The King of the Gnomes sat back on his throne upon the litter and the litter-carriers escorted him away. 'May luck and fortune be on your side, children of Selsior,' he said. 'Farewell.'

The King was then carried down some steps that had been cut in the ground, and were accessible through a large opening in the bottom of a tree trunk. It was soon like the Gnomes had never even been there! They had all gone, and that part of the Forest was empty once again.

'Right,' Lily said as she picked up her rucksack. 'Shall we continue?'

'Are you just pretending that that whole thing didn't happen?' Timothy asked, frustrated.

'No, of course not,' Lily said. 'But we're unharmed, aren't we? We were on their land, and they just wanted to ask us some questions, and they were honouring their arrangement with the Goblins. But the King of the Gnomes relented, they let us go, and now we can be on our way.'

'They were going to feed us to the Wolves!' Timothy retorted.

'They threatened to, yes,' Lily said. 'And I'll confess: I *was* scared for a while there. But the relationships between the creatures of the Forest are very complex.'

'Complex?' Timothy said in disbelief. 'They were going to let us die!'

'I know you were scared, Timothy,' Lily said. 'We all were. Trust me. But that is exactly why we're on this journey, isn't it? To free Selsior, and the Forest, from the rule of the Goblins, so the Gnomes are *not* bribed into handing people over to them, so the Wolves are *not* able to roam around hunting their next meal!'

'I don't want to go any further,' Timothy said.

'No, Timothy, please don't leave us,' Lily said.

'Yes, don't go,' Stephen said.

'Come on, Timothy,' Gregory said. 'Stay.'

'No, I've made up my mind,' Timothy said as he picked up his backpack. 'I want to go back. I'm scared and I want to go home. I want to be with my parents.'

'I can understand that, but there are Wolves in the Forest!' Lily said. 'You shouldn't be on your own, Timothy. Stay with us and you will be safer.'

'I've made up my mind, Lily,' Timothy repeated. 'I'm going back.'

'And that's your call to make,' Lily said. 'I just hope you return home safely.'

'Thank you,' he said. 'Goodbye.'

'Goodbye, Timothy,' Lily, Stephen and Gregory all said.

Timothy put his backpack on and ran south towards Selsior. There were just three members of the group left, who all watched as Timothy soon disappeared from sight.

Lily then turned north. 'Come on,' she said, with sadness in her voice, 'let's go.'

Lily led the way as she and the two boys began the next stage of their mission. If there really was safety in numbers, Lily thought, then she was starting to get worried about the welfare of the group.

Jonathan was fairly sure the coast was clear as he neared the border between the Forest and Selsior. The journey had been a lot longer than he thought it was going to be.

Thwack! A black-armoured arm suddenly appeared from behind a tree and knocked Jonathan out. The Goblin to whom the arm belonged lifted Jonathan over his shoulder and led him to the dungeon in which he would join Matthew. Goblin heads would now roll, as threatened by the Empress...

Chapter 8

SCRATCHES

Lily, Stephen and Gregory were all silent as they continued walking ever further through the Forest. They were distracted by the memories of the boys who had left them: first Matthew, then Jonathan, then Timothy.

When the group had first set out into the Forest, they went with such a great idea of what the journey, the mission, would be like. They were brave heroes venturing into unknown territory, together walking a dangerous path to the destination in the far distance, where they would make a united plea for help. But things had not turned out that way. Three of the boys had decided that they could not continue on the path, feeling that they were not as valiant as their parents had told everybody they were. When there is that much pressure and expectation on your shoulders, it is very easy to buckle under the weight of it all.

Lily could feel that the group was a bit downcast. She looked at Stephen and Gregory and could see the worry and fear on their faces. Their encounter with the Gnomes of the Forest had been very scary, and the shock of it had only just settled in for Lily too. She regretted how blasé she had been about the whole experience with Timothy; but at the time, she had felt that it was her duty to make the group feel calm and relaxed. Maybe she had acted *too* calm and relaxed, Lily now reflected.

Lily turned to Stephen and Gregory with a smile on her face: 'How about some riddles?' she asked.

Stephen shrugged. 'I don't know any riddles,' he said.

'I don't know any either,' Gregory said.

'Don't worry, I'll just set you some!' Lily said enthusiastically.

'Oh, that sounds good,' Stephen said.

'Are they going to be difficult ones?' Gregory asked.

'They may get more difficult as we go along, yes,' Lily said.

'Fair enough,' Gregory said. 'Go ahead!'

'All right... How about this?' Lily said. 'This is a relatively easy one: *What question can you never answer "yes" to?*'

Stephen and Gregory both thought about it for a little while, scratching their heads and stroking their chins.

'Um,' Stephen said. '*What question can you never answer yes to?*' He thought repeating the riddle might help. '*Are you dead?*' he guessed.

'Oh, so close!' Lily said. 'But you couldn't actually answer anything if you were *dead*.'

'*Are you asleep?*' Gregory guessed.

'Yes!' Lily exclaimed.

'Hooray!' Gregory said, punching the air.

'I was so close!' Stephen said, annoyed.

'But not close enough,' Gregory said.

'Don't gloat, Gregory,' Lily said. 'Shall I ask you another one?'

'Yes, go on,' Stephen said.

Lily saw that the two boys were enjoying the challenge of the riddles, although she realised that it had been turned into a competition. As she should have expected, Lily thought.

Lily pointed out some tree roots to Stephen and Gregory which were easy to trip over, and they all stepped carefully over them as they continued walking.

She then carried on with the next riddle: '*No sooner spoken than broken. What is it?*' Lily said.

'*A promise*?' Gregory guessed.

'No,' Lily said.

'Ooh, ooh!' Stephen said, excited. 'Is it *silence*?'

'Yes, it is silence,' Lily said. 'Well done!'

'Oh, darn,' Gregory said. 'Do another one, do another one.'

'All right,' Lily said, 'how about this: *When you have me, you feel like sharing me. But if you do share me, you don't have me. What am I?*'

Stephen whispered the riddle back to himself. He paused after each sentence to think through possible answers. '*...if you do share me, you don't have me...*' he said. '*A secret?*'

'That's the correct answer!' Lily said.

'Yes!' Stephen said.

'You're not giving me a chance to suggest an answer,' Gregory said.

'Well, did you have an answer to suggest to that one?' Stephen asked.

'That's irrelevant,' Gregory said.

'Ready for the next one?' Lily asked.

'Yes,' both of the boys said.

'*You can see nothing else when you look in my face; I will look you in the eye and I will never lie. What am I?*' Lily said.

'*Your reflection,*' Gregory said immediately.

'Correct!' Lily said.

'How did you know that?' Stephen asked Gregory.

'I've heard that one before,' Gregory said.

'Well, that's unfair,' Stephen said.

'It's not my fault I've heard it before and you haven't,' Gregory said.

'Ask the next one please,' Stephen said.

'Hmm, all right,' Lily said. 'Ah, how about this one? It's fairly difficult: *I am not alive, but I grow; I don't have lungs, but I need air; I don't have a mouth, but water kills me. What am I?*'

'That's *really* difficult!' Gregory said. 'How do you remember them?'

'I have a good memory for things like this,' Lily said. 'My mum sets me riddles and puzzles to improve my problem-solving.'

'Shush, shush,' Stephen said. 'I can't think if you're talking...'

'Sorry(!)' Lily said.

'*Water kills me...*' Stephen murmured under his breath. 'Oh, it's *fire*!'

'It is fire, yes!' Lily said.

'Oh, darn!' Gregory said.

'Ha-ha! That makes it 3-2 to me,' Stephen said smugly.

'It's not supposed to be a competition,' Lily said. 'It's supposed to pass the time, to keep us positive and to cheer us up! I thought we were all feeling a bit blue.'

'Yes, I was feeling a bit blue,' Gregory said.

'It was a good idea to ask us riddles to cheer us up, Lily,' Stephen said. 'Could you ask another one?'

'Yes, all right,' Lily said. 'This is the most difficult riddle I know: *This old one runs forever, but never moves at all. He has not lungs nor throat, but still a mighty roaring call. What is it?*'

'Oh, my goodness,' Gregory said. 'That is really hard.'

'I warned you!' Lily said.

'Some type of animal?' Stephen asked.

'No,' Lily said.

'A creature?' Gregory asked. 'One of the creatures of the Forest?'

'No,' Lily said again.

The two boys thought in silence for a few moments, but both of them soon realised that they were stumped. This last riddle was simply too fiendish for them to solve!

'Oh, I have no idea,' Stephen said.

'Me neither,' Gregory said. 'Tell us the answer.'

'Yes, tell us the answer!' Stephen said.

'It's *a waterfall,*' Lily said.

'Ohhh!' Gregory said. 'I would never have got that.'

'I could have done if I'd had a little more time,' Stephen said.

'Sure(!)' Gregory said.

'Now, now, let's not bicker amongst ourselves,' Lily said, 'Anyway, that's the last of the riddles!'

'Oh,' Stephen said, disappointed. 'Thank you for asking us riddles – they were good brain teasers and they have kept us entertained on the journey!'

'You are very clever, Lily,' Gregory said. 'If you didn't know that already. And very kind. I'm so glad you are here with us in the Forest. It would be a more dangerous place without you, and a lot less fun.'

'Gregory...' Lily said, not knowing what to say in response. 'That's, uh, some of the kindest things anyone has ever said to me. Thank you.'

'I echo everything Gregory said, by the way,' Stephen said.

'Well, thank you, both of you,' Lily said. 'And I'm glad that you are both here with me on this journey.'

Stephen and Gregory both smiled at Lily, and she smiled back. Lily exhaled as she faced forward and refocused solely on the journey through the Forest.

They had been walking for a while when it became obvious to the whole group that they needed a rest. Lily saw a stream up ahead, running from west to east, and thought it would be a nice spot to take a break, so they could watch the peaceful flow of water. There was something about the sight and sound of a babbling brook which caused a tranquil and soothing feeling in Lily's soul.

While Lily and Stephen sat on a couple of tree logs overlooking the stream, Gregory went right towards the stream to take some sips of water. As he was quenching his thirst, he saw a frog minding its own business, croaking and catching flies with its long tongue if they had the misfortune to buzz past at the wrong moment.

'Ribbit,' Gregory said to the frog. 'Ribbit!'

The frog turned and hopped away from Gregory. Gregory tried not to feel rejected as his brief amphibian companion disappeared upstream. It was by looking upstream that Gregory noticed two Wolves sipping water themselves. The Wolves had grey shaggy fur, a long tail, a broad snout, and *very* sharp teeth.

'Do not move, Gregory,' Gregory told himself. 'And do not make a sound. If they don't see you, they won't attack you.'

Gregory had found a reasonably sensible approach, but he could not predict what Stephen was going to do. Stephen had not seen the Wolves upstream, so he ran up behind Gregory and splashed water in his face.

'Water fight!' Stephen announced gleefully.

'Wolves!' Gregory yelled, pointing in their direction.

Lily, who had been sitting reading her book, stood up and saw for herself the Goblins' canine hunters, who were now looking alert and eyeing their prey.

'Argh!' Stephen screamed, before fleeing as fast as his legs would carry him.

Gregory started to run as well, more slowly than Stephen, as the Wolves growled loudly and followed the two boys in pursuit. Lily had not been seen by the Wolves. She got her backpack on her shoulders, but she was still carrying her book as she attempted to catch up with the boys and the predators. The gleaming sunlight bounced off the cover of the book into Lily's eyes, making it a struggle to see where she was going.

Lily then tried to find the right information in her book about how to deal with the Wolves. When the King of the Gnomes had mentioned the Wolves before, Lily was almost certain that she had not read about them in her book. But she thought, most likely in vain, that there might have been a snippet of information somewhere that could help her stop the Wolves eating Stephen and Gregory, or taking them back to Selsior into the hands of their Goblin masters.

Lily was soon out of breath as she desperately flicked through the pages of the book, while simultaneously looking down to avoid tripping as she ran between the trees. Stephen and Gregory were leading the Wolves further and further through the Forest – they were doing a good job of outrunning their hunters.

Lily looked up and saw that there were scratches that had been made high up on the tree trunks surrounding her, with the bark exposed. She saw that they were not there by accident – they seemed to have some sort of design to them. She turned over some pages in her book, to try to find any clues as to the reason behind these deliberate scratches in the tree trunks.

'Scratches in the trees, scratches in the trees,' she muttered as she scanned the content of the pages.

Lily realised that she had found the right paragraph in the right section. She looked up again at the scratches in the tree trunks, and gasped! This part of the Forest was the territory of a rather tall kind of creatures...

Up ahead, the Wolves were still chasing Stephen and Gregory, when two large human-looking fists appeared from behind some trees and bashed the Wolves on their heads, knocking them unconscious. What impeccable timing!

Stephen and Gregory turned around and walked back towards the Wolves to see what had happened, when they were seized by the same two hands which had knocked out the Wolves and tightly clasped by them. Lily caught up and she was seized by a third hand and tightly clasped as well.

The hands the three of them were trapped in started to squeeze them firmly – so firmly in fact that they thought their heads were going to pop off their shoulders like corks from bottles! Lily, Stephen and Gregory saw who the hands belonged to: three Giants. They were twelve foot tall, muscular, bare-chested, wearing just dark grey shorts which were torn and grubby; and they had long, thin and wispy black hair and short beards. They each inspected the children they were squeezing, as if they were a peculiar new species which they had never seen before.

Although the Giants were quite threatening and were actually causing them quite a bit of discomfort by squeezing them, Lily, Stephen and Gregory were actually not that afraid of them; instead they were just grateful that the Giants had prevented the Wolves from either devouring them or carrying them in their jaws to the Goblins.

'Thank you for saving us from the Wolves!' Gregory said.

Another Giant stepped forward and looked at the children. 'Good afternoon, children,' he said. 'I am the Lord of the Giants, at your service.' And as he said "at your service", the Lord of the Giants bowed, which none of the children was expecting. He continued: 'Can I ask who you are, where you are from, where you are going, and what you are doing?'

'That's a lot of questions, Your Lordship!' Lily said. 'I would be able to answer them all fully if we were not being squeezed.'

'Release your grasp around them,' the Lord of the Giants said, 'but do not let them go.'

The Giants did as they were told and Lily, Stephen and Gregory all breathed a sigh of relief.

'We are children from the Kingdom of Selsior,' Lily began as usual. 'My name is Lily and my companions are called Stephen and Gregory. Your Lordship, we are on a journey through the Forest, to the Land of Zelnia on the other side, to ask the Witch there to help the people of Selsior defeat the Goblins and to reclaim their homeland.'

'Hmm,' the Lord of the Giants said, 'that story does sound a little bit far-fetched to me.' He turned to the other Giants: 'Does it sound far-fetched to you?'

The other Giants nodded in agreement, and inspected each of the children closely again, and breath from the Giants' nostrils felt like wind on the children's faces.

'I mean, why would the people of Selsior send *children*?' the Lord of the Giants asked.

'They sent us because the Magical Folk respond to children more,' Lily said, 'because of their innocence, and their open-mindedness to magic and mystery.'

'Hmm, I still doubt your story,' the Lord of the Giants said. 'It is more plausible that you are actually working for the Goblins. You were more likely patrolling the Forest alongside those Wolves, rather than running away from them, as it may have initially appeared.'

'No, Your Lordship, I assure you that we are not Goblins,' Lily said.

The Lord of the Giants chuckled, then he wiped his mouth and nose. 'I did not suggest that you *were* Goblins,' he said, chuckling again, 'just that you were *working* for them.'

'Oh, it was just a silly mistake on my part!' Lily said, not believing that she had made such a silly mistake at such a critical time. 'I meant to say "I assure you that we are not *working for* the Goblins". I really did. Please believe me.'

'Was it just a slip of the tongue or did it betray a deeper truth?' the Lord of the Giants asked. 'I am now of a mind to suspect that you really *are* Goblins – Goblins in disguise. In a very good disguise, I would admit.'

Stephen and Gregory looked at each other, worried. They did not like where this was going. What would the Giants do to the children if they really believed them to be Goblins in disguise? Nothing good, they were certain of that – Goblins were not exactly popular in the Forest. The two boys were worried that the Giants were one kind of creatures that Lily was not going to be able to reason with and help them get out of their clutches. If Lily could not save the day, then who could?

'I have an idea, Your Lordship,' one of the other three Giants said.

'Yes?' the Lord of the Giants said.

'We could try taking off the outer skin to see if they are Goblins underneath,' the Giant said.

'Whoa, whoa, whoa!' Lily yelled. 'There is no need for that, we promise you. We are not Goblins!'

'Yes, there is no need for that,' Gregory said.

'No, none at all,' Stephen said.

'Look, I can show you,' Lily said. She pulled on her skin to show that it was not a layer of any disguise covering real Goblin skin. 'You see, this is really my skin! We are not Goblins masquerading as human children. They happen to be a lot taller than us anyway...'

'You could be Goblin *children* masquerading as human children,' the Giant said, the one who had come up with the idea of taking off the children's outer skin.

'Yes, that is true,' another Giant said.

'But we're not!' Lily said very impatiently. 'So can we *please* just give this a rest?'

'You really are on this journey you talked about?' the Lord of the Giants said.

'Yes, we are on a journey to talk to the Witch in Zelnia,' Lily said, 'in order to ask her to remove the Goblins from power in the Kingdom of Selsior. That is our task. And we are so close to achieving it, so please don't stop us in our tracks now. We beg you.'

'There will be no begging required,' the Lord of the Giants said. 'We believe you now. We just needed to investigate. We have never seen people in here, you see. We have seen Wizards and Witches, but not non-magical people.'

'You've seen the Magical Folk in the Forest?' Lily asked.

'Oh, yes,' the Lord of the Giants said, 'the Wizards and Witches would come in here from time to time when they all lived in the Land of Zelnia. When they moved away from the Ancient Woodland in the West, they were planning to make their new home here in the Forest, but they found that it was *occupied*. So after they had settled in Zelnia, they would just make visits into the Forest, because they felt that all of the trees in The World had something magic about them.'

'Do you know why the Magical Folk did move away from the Ancient Woodland in the West?' Lily asked. 'I've never understood that part. Could you shed any light on it?'

'Yes, I have heard the story,' the Lord of the Giants said. 'There was an excellent Wizard child prodigy called Zaan. He was very intelligent, gifted in fact, and it was foretold that he would be one of the best Wizards the Magical Folk would ever produce.

'But as Zaan grew older, he began to be consumed by the desire for power. And he succumbed to that desire: he attempted to topple the leaders of the Magical Folk and become the king, or emperor, or some other type of ruler. The leaders managed to stop him though, and they cast him into exile.

'But before he departed, Zaan put a curse on the Woodland, which meant that nothing could grow. There was no light or life, and the Magical Folk's existence became very miserable indeed. Unsustainable. So they realised that they had to move away from there.'

'So how, why, did the Magical Folk return to the Woodland in the West after they had been banished from Selsior to the Land of Zelnia?' Lily asked.

'Well, it was during the years after their banishment from the Kingdom of Selsior that they finally hunted down the Malevolent Wizard Zaan,' the Lord of the Giants said, 'walking along a lake-shore far away in the east.'

'And what did they do with him?' Lily asked, although she was fairly sure that she already knew the answer to her question.

'They executed him right there and then, on the spot,' the Lord of the Giants said, confirming Lily's suspicion. 'They chopped off his head, to be absolutely certain that he was dead. They took his head and his body back to the Enchanted Lands and buried them in the Serene Sea. And thus Zaan's curse on the Woodland was lifted.'

'I see,' Lily said, feeling a tad ill. She had always been a bit squeamish when there was talk of death, especially murder as she had just heard about. 'Well, thank you for informing us of all that...'

'You are very welcome,' the Lord of the Giants said. 'And *thank you* for going on the journey to find the Witch in the Land of Zelnia. We have not seen her ourselves for many years now, I am sad to say. I do hope she helps you to defeat those atrocious Goblins.'

'You have had run-ins with the Goblins, I assume?' Lily asked.

'We have lived in the Forest for hundreds of years now,' the Lord of the Giants said. 'But we come from elsewhere. You see, we were the first creatures to inhabit The World. And we used to rule the lands. But when the humans arrived, they attacked and killed many of us. Those of us who survived fled into the places in The World where we could hide and live in peace. And my kin dwelt here in the Forest for many years in peace.

'Then the Goblins came from the east. They invaded and conquered the Forest, and they chose to rule it with malice and hatred. They used to ambush us in large numbers, so they could overpower us when they felt like attacking us and ridiculing us. They would knock us to the ground, bind our hands and feet, and jump around on our chests or backs to assert their dominance and control.'

'That's awful!' Lily said. 'And the Goblins are just as cruel to the people of Selsior. You can see why we want to free ourselves from them!'

'Yes, I can see why,' the Lord of the Giants said. 'You know, I have noticed that ever since you first encountered us, you have not really been afraid of us. You were bothered by my kin squeezing you earlier, but you have not expressed any trepidation.'

'Well, the Goblins attacked you because you were different from them and bigger than them, and they attacked you because they *feared* you,' Lily said. 'But as you saved my friends, by so helpfully knocking out those Wolves which were chasing them, I felt there was no need or reason to fear you, and I'm sure my friends would agree.'

Lily turned to Stephen and Gregory, as did the Lord of the Giants. The two boys nodded exuberantly, and smiled at all of the Giants. What the Lord of Giants had said was certainly true. Despite the Giants being intimidating, and holding the group quite tightly in their hands the entire time, Stephen and Gregory had not really feared for their lives. They even remained reasonably unafraid when they were being accused of being Goblin spies, or of being actual Goblins, and when there had been talk of the Giants pulling their skin off!

'The Giants are very appreciative of your kindness,' the Lord of the Giants said. 'The World would be a better place if everyone was as kind as you, children from Selsior. I said earlier that there would be no begging required, but *I* now beg *you* to succeed in your task.

'The Forest has been free from Goblins for twelve years now, and it has become a much better place to live. I hope for your sake that you can do the same for the Kingdom of Selsior. And I hope, for *our* sake, that you will not simply let them come back here, and that you will somehow get rid of them once and for all.'

'We will try our best, Your Lordship,' Lily said.

The Giants placed the children on the ground. The Lord of the Giants bowed once more, before leading his kin away. Lily was surprised by how quietly the Giants walked, considering their height and weight. No wonder she never heard them coming when the Wolves were chasing Stephen and Gregory, Lily thought.

Thinking about the Wolves, she turned to see the Wolves still lying unconscious on the Forest floor. Lily found it amusing how innocent and harmless the Wolves looked while they lay there, as if asleep, when not that long ago they were eagerly pursuing Stephen and Gregory with their eyes ablaze and their jaws open wide.

'I'm going home,' Stephen suddenly announced.

'What?' Gregory asked. 'Why? We've come so far now, Stephen.'

'I want to go before the Wolves wake up,' Stephen said. 'I don't want to be chased by them again. I don't want to be caught by them and ripped apart, or led into the clutches of the Goblins.'

'But we are too close to the northern side of the Forest now for you to go all the way back to Selsior,' Lily argued.

'But the Wolves will assume that we went further north into the Forest, rather than south,' Stephen countered, 'so if we go back, the Wolves will not find us.'

'What do you mean "we", Stephen?' Lily asked.

'We should *all* go back to Selsior,' Stephen said firmly. 'Those Wolves are going to wake up and they are going to hunt us and they are going to *kill* us! Now I don't know about you, but I really don't want to die here. I don't want to be a martyr. I'm aware we are on this really important and really noble mission to find the Witch in Zelnia, but I personally don't think the mission is worth all of us losing our lives...' He paused for a moment. 'I am young, and I've got the rest of my life to live! So I'm going back, and I hope you are wise enough, and sensible enough, to join me on the journey home.'

'We must achieve this mission, Stephen,' Lily said. 'We are so close, and I'm not going to give up now. I would never forgive myself.'

'I'm not going to give up now either,' Gregory said.

'It's your choice,' Stephen said, shaking his head. 'Look, even if you don't think the Wolves are enough of a threat to abort the mission, what if there is some other kind of creatures in here that won't let you pass? What are you going to do then?'

'The Giants are the last creatures we're going to meet before reaching the northern edge of the Forest!' Lily said. 'It says so in my–'

'Yes, in your book,' Stephen interjected. 'I know, I know. But what if the author of your amazing book has got it wrong? What if there aren't just Fairies, Bats, Gnomes and Giants in here? What if there is something, or a whole group of something, that you don't know about, that you haven't read about? What will you do then?'

'We would make it through, one way or another,' Lily said. 'But I assure you that the path is clear now. We just have to get to Zelnia. And that is all.'

'You're not going to change my mind, Lily,' Stephen said. He turned away and started to walk south. He then turned back to face Lily and Gregory. 'I wish I could have gone with you to the end.'

'You pretty much have,' Lily said with an affectionate smile. 'Goodbye, Stephen.'

'Goodbye, Lily,' Stephen said. 'Goodbye, Gregory.'

'Farewell,' Gregory said.

Stephen turned south and started to run.

It was just Lily and Gregory now. Lily looked at Gregory and reflected on how much he had changed since she met him the day before in the Forest, when he was with Matthew, Jonathan, Timothy and Stephen. He had been the quietest and the most withdrawn of the group. But as time had gone on, he had slowly come out of his shell and he had flourished as a member of the group. And she was not just thinking that because he had been so complimentary to her! After all, while the other four boys had decided against continuing on their journey through the Forest, Gregory had loyally stuck by Lily, and he now seemed intent on seeing the task completed.

Lily motioned to Gregory that it was time to continue on their journey, leaving the Wolves to their slumber.

Chapter 9

ALMOST THERE

In Selsior, life was extremely tough and harsh, both for the people and for some of the Goblins, believe it or not. The Empress of the Goblins had kept her promise and ordered the beheading of the Goblins whose duty it was to patrol the edge of the Forest, for singularly failing in their duty.

Matthew, Jonathan and Timothy had all been captured on the border and locked up in the Goblin dungeons. So the Goblins knew for certain now that a group of boys had entered the Forest without them knowing about it.

The Empress sent out a decree far and wide across the Kingdom, saying that if someone gave up whoever it was who had sent the boys into the Forest, the informant would be rewarded, while the "traitor" or "*traitors*" would be punished. But nobody came forward offering to lure the person, or people, responsible into the Goblins' trap.

In the decree, the Goblins had provided detailed descriptions of the children – a consequence of this was that their parents found out which of them had returned and been captured by the Goblins, and which of them were still in the Forest somewhere.

Lily's parents were convinced that their daughter was dead. Agatha wept hour after hour, while Benjamin tried to stay strong for the sake of Edwin and Hilary. Benjamin and Agatha imagined that something terrible had happened in the Forest: one of the kinds of creatures – either the Fairies, the Bats, the Gnomes, or the Giants – had attacked the children, and Matthew, Jonathan and Timothy had run back to Selsior while Stephen and Gregory had run in other directions. It was impossible that Lily could have survived an attack by any of those creatures, Benjamin and Agatha thought.

As none of the other people in Selsior knew that Lily had gone into the Forest with the five boys, they whispered to each other that all of their hopes now rested in Stephen's and Gregory's fate. They did not know yet that Stephen was on his way back to Selsior too.

Stephen's and Gregory's parents bragged about their boys' bravery and determination in the face of danger. They boasted that while Matthew, Jonathan and Timothy had obviously got too scared and given up on the mission, their boys had enough courage and love for their homeland to accomplish the mission, no matter what.

The parents of Matthew, Jonathan and Timothy, on the other hand, were both disappointed about their sons' decisions to extract themselves from the group, and devastated that their sons were currently languishing in the Goblin dungeons.

In the Palace of the Empress of the Goblins, a couple of Goblin generals walked timidly into the Throne Room and towards their leader. The generals knew that the Empress was not in the best of moods, so they were wary of causing her to be even angrier and to ask for *their* heads as well. They also knew the subject upon which the Empress had become fixated, obsessed about even, causing her to have sleepless nights.

The two Goblin generals saluted the Empress.

'You called for us, Your Imperial Majesty?' one of the generals asked.

'Yes, I did,' the Empress said. 'I want to know what you are doing about these children in the Forest.'

'We sent a couple of Wolves in, Your Imperial Majesty,' the general said, 'to look for any more children and bring them here to the Palace.'

'Have they come back with anyone?' the Empress asked.

'No, not yet,' the general said. 'We were going to give them some more time.'

'We might not have *more time*!' the Empress bellowed. 'Despatch a whole pack of Wolves to hunt down any child in there. And instruct the Wolves to bring them directly to me so they can stand trial for treason against their Empress and be *executed*!'

'Yes, Your Imperial Majesty,' the general said.

'I know why they have sent children into the Forest by the way,' the Empress said.

'Why?' the other general asked. The Empress looked at him and raised an eyebrow. 'I mean, why, *Your Imperial Majesty*?' The general knew that the Empress cared a great deal about respect, and the Empress being addressed with the correct title was a big part of that.

'These children have been sent into the Forest to reach the Land of Zelnia on the other side,' the Empress said, 'because the people of Selsior hope to make contact with the remnants of the Magical Folk. They are the only ones who have defeated us before, when we first attempted to invade the Kingdom of Selsior. Now the people of the Kingdom are trying to get them on their side again.'

The Empress paused for a few moments, and the Goblin generals looked at each other awkwardly, worrying that the Empress was becoming paranoid.

'The children must not be allowed to reach the other side of the Forest,' the Empress continued. 'The Magical Folk are the only ones stronger and more powerful than us. If they did come to the aid of the people of Selsior, we might be defeated and overthrown...'

The Empress rose from her throne and stood commandingly in front of the generals, pointing a finger at them both.

'And I will not let that happen!' the Empress shouted. 'It was under *my* leadership that the Goblins invaded and conquered the greatest of the Fourteen Realms, and I am not going to have that achievement taken away from me now! The people of Selsior will rue the day they conspired against me! Do you hear me?'

'Yes, Your Imperial Majesty,' the generals both said as they saluted.

'Why are you still here then?' the Empress screamed. 'Go! Go now!'

The Goblin generals hurriedly turned and fled from the Throne Room. They looked at each other as they ran, terrified.

'Unleash the Wolves! Bring the children to me alive!' the Empress ordered as she sat back on her throne. 'Burn the Forest down to ashes if you have to! Whatever it takes to find those children! Just do not fail me!'

Lily and Gregory were both feeling a little weary as the sun began to set in the West. *The West.* Lily thought about the Wizards and Witches in the Ancient Woodland in the West, in the rolling hills of the Enchanted Lands, and wondered what their lives were like back in their ancestral homeland.

Lily had not known about the curse of the fallen Wizard Zaan, which the Lord of the Giants had told her about. It was not featured in the book that she possessed – perhaps it was the story of another book that the author had written, Lily thought.

Anyhow, Lily was happy that the Magical Folk had been able to reclaim *their* homeland – she just hoped that her people would soon do the same, with the Witch's help of course.

'Shall we have a rest, Gregory?' Lily asked.

'I thought you'd never ask!' Gregory said. 'I thought you were going to try and walk without stopping as our journey is nearing its end.'

'Oh, no, I definitely need to have a rest now,' Lily said.

Lily walked over to a tree log, which she noticed was still a bit wet from the rain the night before. She took off her raincoat and laid it down on the log before sitting on it. Gregory, meanwhile, walked over and just sat on it, without a care in the world!

'My bottom feels a bit damp now,' Gregory said matter-of-factly.

'Yes, it's because the tree log is wet!' Lily said, suppressing laughter.

'Oh,' Gregory said. 'Never mind.'

Lily rummaged around in her rucksack. 'I think I've got a chocolate brownie in here somewhere,' she said, 'if I remember rightly. Here it is!'

She took a small tin out, removed the lid, and picked up the chocolate brownie inside. She tore the brownie in half and offered a piece to Gregory.

'Oh, thank you very much,' Gregory said, taking the piece and eating it straight away. 'Yummy! That's delicious, that is.'

'My mum made them,' Lily said, taking a bite of her own piece of brownie.

'She is a very good baker!' Gregory said.

'She is indeed,' Lily said.

Gregory looked around in his backpack and got his own tin out. He removed the lid and inside there was a small apple cake. He took out two slices and offered one to Lily.

'Thank you,' Lily said, taking a bite. 'That's yummy too.'

'My mum is a very good baker too,' Gregory said, eating his slice in one bite. 'Yes, that was very nice. Good sustenance!'

'Yes, that should give us enough fuel for the last leg of the journey,' Lily said.

There were a few moments of silence, as Lily ate the rest of her slice of cake and Gregory looked thoughtfully into the distance. After she swallowed the very last bit, Lily turned to Gregory.

'Gregory, can I ask you a difficult question?' she said.

'Um, yes, if you'd like to,' Gregory said.

'Did any of you – I mean Matthew, Jonathan, Timothy, Stephen and yourself – did any of you really want to embark on this journey?' Lily asked.

'I think we all *thought* we wanted to go on the journey,' Gregory said. 'We thought it would be a bit of a laugh, a bit of a jolly, walking through the Forest and asking the Witch in Zelnia for help against the Goblins...' He paused, then continued: 'But when we realised how dangerous it might be, and how serious it was, we all started to doubt ourselves. With your dad telling us about what we might encounter in here, and advising us to leave each other behind if any of us or some of us got into trouble or peril – it scared the living daylights out of us, to be honest!'

'Yes, I can imagine,' Lily said.

'And all of our parents sort of pressured us into going too, I would say,' Gregory continued. 'They were all so excited about the notion of the five of us going on this brave journey, this brave quest. They did not really think about the...'

'The implications,' Lily said, helping Gregory out.

'Yes, the implications,' Gregory repeated. 'I mean, we are still only young, Stephen was the oldest and he was still only thirteen-years-old... And we were being sent on this journey through a very dangerous Forest, which would have been a lot more dangerous if you had not been here, Lily. I don't know what we would have done without you.' His eyes widened as he speculated: 'We might have been drowned by the Fairies, or had our blood sucked out of our bodies by the Bats, or fed to the Goblins' Wolves by the Gnomes, or squashed like ants by the Giants...'

Lily giggled. 'Yes, you may have a point there,' she said.

'So why were you so determined to go?' Gregory asked. 'Why put yourself in such danger? Was it just that you had the book with the answers, or was there something else?'

'Good question,' Lily said. 'Well, I actually came up with the idea of a group of children going through the Forest and appealing to the Witch in Zelnia.'

'It was your idea?' Gregory asked. 'I did not know that.'

'Well, the men of the Kingdom would not have told you,' Lily said. 'But they dismissed my idea the first time around because they just wanted to fight the Goblins in battle. But when the battle happened and the Goblins won, they thought again, and listened to my idea with a lot more understanding and interest. And they decided it was the right way to go about rescuing Selsior.' She paused. 'But then my dad told me that I couldn't be one of the children who went through, because it could only really be boys. And I was devastated. So I snuck out of my room to join you.'

'You've told me *how* you joined us on the journey,' Gregory said, 'but not *why*.'

'The reason *why* I joined you is because I wanted to play my part in saving the Kingdom of Selsior from the Goblins,' Lily said. 'I spent my whole childhood wondering how I could help to get rid of them. I felt that it was my burden, to free my people.'

'Why?' Gregory asked.

'I don't know,' Lily said. 'It has just always felt like it was. I can't explain it. But then I bought the book and read it from cover to cover, and I knew that I had found the way. The people of Selsior had seemed to completely forget about the Magical Folk, and not give them any thought at all. But I knew they were the answer. I knew this Witch was the answer.'

'I used to think about the part I could play in the rescue of Selsior too when I was younger,' Gregory said.

'Oh, did you?' Lily said enthusiastically. 'What did you imagine you'd be doing?'

'I thought I'd be a brave soldier,' Gregory said, 'a noble warrior leading a great military force against the Goblins on horseback. Or sometimes I saw myself riding on the back of a dragon! We were soaring through the air like one of the great birds of prey – an eagle, or a hawk, or a falcon! And the dragon would breathe fire over the entire Goblin army! My imagination did occasionally run a bit wild...'

'Just a bit!' Lily said.

'I never imagined that the mission to free the Kingdom of Selsior would be a few of us walking through this Forest,' Gregory said, 'and that there would just be two of us left by the time we reached the Land of Zelnia.'

'Are you definitely sure you want to carry on?' Lily asked. 'I want to give you the opportunity to say you don't want to continue on the journey and go home.'

'No, I don't want to leave,' Gregory said. 'I want to keep going; I want to see the mission accomplished. I also don't want to disappoint my parents...'

'Gregory, that shouldn't be one of the reasons you do this,' Lily said.

'I know, but it is,' he said. 'Besides, I figure it's safer with you than without you. I've certainly learnt that lesson!'

'You must stop with your flattery, Gregory,' Lily said blushingly.

'All right, I will,' Gregory said.

Lily looked away and Gregory looked down at his feet, feeling awkward. The truth was that since they had been alone, Gregory had started to like Lily a lot – he liked her as more than just a friend. He had never met anyone like her before. He admired Lily's intelligence and her courage, and she was also the kindest person he had ever known. Gregory hoped that when this was all over, he and Lily would at least have a long-lasting friendship.

'I need a drink!' Lily said, rummaging around in her rucksack again. 'I've got a bottle of water in here somewhere.'

Lily found the glass bottle she had packed and took three big gulps of water.

'Ah!' Lily said. 'Lovely water. It's managed to keep cool.'

'I just remembered that my mum packed a flask of tea for me,' Gregory said, trying to find the flask in his backpack.

'How much did your mum pack for your journey?' Lily asked.

'Quite a lot,' Gregory said, chuckling. He brought a metallic flask out of his backpack and took off the lid.

'That tea is not going to be warm,' Lily said.

Gregory took a sip of the tea. 'Bleurgh!' Gregory exclaimed. 'It's tepid. I want to heat it up, so it doesn't go to waste.'

Lily thought for a few moments. She looked at her glass bottle and took a mouthful of water. She looked at it again and had a brainwave. She went around collecting as many twigs and sticks as she could find and put them into a pile on the ground.

'What are you doing?' Gregory asked.

'I'm going to heat up your tea,' Lily responded.

Lily then looked up at the sky, and held her glass bottle in exactly the right spot where the sun was shining through the bottle and onto the twigs and sticks on the Forest floor. Nothing happened. Lily checked the location of the sun again and held the bottle in the right place.

'I see what you're trying to do there, Lily,' Gregory said, 'but that won't work with normal glass. You need a magnifying glass.'

'Oh,' Lily said. Lily was very clever, and her gifts lay in literature and history, but science was certainly not her strong suit! She put the glass bottle down on the ground, despondent.

'It's lucky then that I have a magnifying glass,' Gregory said.

'What? Why?' Lily asked.

'My mum packed it in case there was anything in the Forest I wanted to examine closely –

bees and butterflies and suchlike,' Gregory said. 'That hasn't happened so far.'

'Oh, brilliant, Gregory!' Lily said. 'You're brilliant! Your mum is brilliant!'

Gregory got the magnifying glass out of his backpack and joined Lily on the Forest floor. He held the magnifying glass in the perfect spot so the sunlight went through it and made a bright dot on one of the sticks in the pile. After a few moments, the end of the stick was ignited and a fire was lit. Success!

Lily and Gregory let the fire grow for a few minutes. Lily was aware that the two of them had been stationary for quite a long time, but she knew that they were so close to the end of the journey through the Forest that there was no problem having an extended break from walking.

Once the fire was large and strong enough, Gregory held the bottom of his flask over the flames to warm up the cold liquid within. He did this for a little while, then opened the flask and took a tiny sip.

'Hmm,' Gregory said. 'Warm enough! Do you want some tea, Lily?'

'Ooh, yes, please,' Lily said, 'there's nothing in The World like warm tea.' She took a sip. 'Lukewarm tea is the second best thing in The World...' She smiled at Gregory, then gave his flask back to him.

Gregory drank the rest of his tea, while Lily finished off her bottle of water.

'Right,' Lily said. 'We should go.'

Gregory packed away the flask and the magnifying glass, and they both set off for the last stage of their trek through the Forest.

They had been walking for about an hour when Lily noticed that the Forest was going to come to an end in a hundred metres or so. There was a narrow, wooden gated bridge over a river at the edge of the Forest, and there were no more trees once the bridge had been crossed.

'Look, Gregory!' Lily said elatedly. 'The bridge marks the northern side of the Forest. We made it! It's the Land of Zelnia on the other side of the bridge.'

'I never thought I'd see the end of the Forest!' Gregory said.

Lily and Gregory ran towards the bridge and Lily opened the gate. Then they walked across the bridge, somewhat nervously, as if it might suddenly give way beneath their feet, or as if it was not physically there, but an illusion created by the Magical Folk to stop uninvited visitors from entering their land.

The two children left the Forest for good and now stood in another place entirely.

'Behold, Gregory: the Land of Zelnia, the former home of the Magical Folk of the West,' Lily announced.

Lily and Gregory looked around at the land in front of them. Lily had read that the Land of Zelnia used to be populous, with houses dotted around in which the Magical Folk lived; there were farms where animals were raised, and fields where crops were cultivated; and magic lessons took place in the school.

But the land Lily and Gregory saw now was very different indeed: it was abandoned, the grass was overgrown, and the buildings had fallen into varying degrees of ruin. There were no crops in the field, only a handful of sheep, cows, pigs and chickens grazing in the farm, and there was a barn in the distance that looked barely used. There was a clear view of rugged mountains on the horizon, far away in the Highlands of Zelnia; mist formed a mask around the tall peaks.

'This is where the Magical Folk came back to live after they were banished from Selsior by the King and Queen,' Lily told Gregory. 'But as the years passed, many Wizards and Witches returned to the Ancient Woodland in the West, within the Enchanted Lands by the Serene Sea. But this one Witch decided to stay. She is thought to be towards the end of her life, which is why it's imperative that we talk to her as soon as possible.'

'We'd better get going then,' Gregory said.

'Indeed,' Lily said. 'Let's have a look around.'

Lily and Gregory walked forwards and started to inspect the first house they came across. They looked inside the window and saw some possessions lying around. Lily went up to the front door of the house and tried the doorknob. The door was unlocked. She opened it and stepped inside. Gregory walked in behind Lily and closed the door.

Inside, Lily and Gregory entered the living room, where there was a wand left on the mantlepiece and a couple of broomsticks leaning against a wall. Lily had a look around, while Gregory picked up the wand and pointed it strongly at the front window. Nothing happened obviously, because he was not a Wizard! He then put the wand back on the mantlepiece, and followed Lily as she walked out of the living room into the kitchen.

Lily looked at the cupboards and the stove. Some of the cupboards had been left empty from where the magical occupants had quickly grabbed supplies before leaving the Land of Zelnia.

Gregory entered the kitchen and saw a fireplace opposite the cupboards and stove. He walked towards it and noticed that there was a cauldron still hanging on a hook in the fireplace. He stepped onto the hearth and looked inside the cauldron to see if there was any mixture left. It was empty – he was disappointed.

As Gregory turned away, his backpack caught some pans hanging on the side of the fireplace. They fell onto the tiled floor with a resounding crash. Lily gasped. As he reacted to the crash, Gregory lurched backwards and knocked the cauldron off its hook, which made yet another loud noise as it hit the floor. The sound reverberated in the fireplace and up the chimney.

Gregory went red in the face from embarrassment. There was a screeching of cats in the distance, which scared Lily and Gregory, but also gave them hope because it meant that there was life nearby.

'Gregory!' Lily said sternly, like a teacher telling off a naughty pupil.

'Sorry,' Gregory said with his eyes cast down.

'Let's go outside,' Lily said. 'Maybe the cats can lead us to the Witch.'

'Good idea,' Gregory said, trying to win back Lily's favour.

They walked briskly out of the house and saw a clowder of cats moving slowly towards them, almost threateningly. The cats were black with white streaks; they purred and meowed in unison, and they sniffed the air as they caught the new scents of the two non-magical visitors. The cats encircled Lily and Gregory, and got closer and closer to them.

'Lily,' Gregory said, 'I know they're small but I'm actually quite scared.'

'It's fine,' Lily said, 'just don't make any sudden movements.'

Lily and Gregory then heard a voice come from nowhere, in a language they could not understand. The cats all turned together and ran off into a house a few metres away, and its door was slammed shut.

'That's where the Witch must be!' Lily said joyfully. She went to run in the direction of the house, but saw that Gregory did not move at all.

'Are you all right?' Lily asked him.

'I don't want to go in there,' Gregory said.

'Why?' Lily asked. 'You have nothing to fear now, Gregory. The worst of it is over. We just need to meet the Witch and ask her to come and help the people of Selsior. That's what we're here for.' She walked to him and took Gregory's hand in hers.

'Come on. The mission is almost over. Let's finish it together.'

'It should just be you, Lily,' Gregory said. 'I'm just going to get in the way and make some other clumsy mistake. You don't need me by your side.'

'Gregory…' Lily said.

'You can handle this alone,' Gregory said. 'Ever since we started this, it was obvious it was going to be you talking to the Witch single-handedly. You were always going to do this part on your own.'

'I don't have to,' Lily said sadly. 'You could talk to her with me.'

'I think the Witch will respond better if it's just you,' Gregory said. 'I believe in you, Lily. I have complete and utter trust in you.'

'All right, don't over-egg it,' Lily said.

Gregory withdrew his hand from Lily's and walked backwards. 'Do us all proud. Save the Kingdom! Save the people!' he said. He then turned and ran towards the Forest.

Before too long, Gregory disappeared from sight. Lily hoped he would be all right going through the Forest back to Selsior. She looked forward to seeing him again.

Lily turned and walked towards the house into which the cats had gone. It was now time for her to talk to the Witch.

Chapter 10

ALONE

Lily was now on her own in the Land of Zelnia. She never really thought it would come to this; she imagined that she would be with a whole group of children who would make their case to the Witch together. But the responsibility had now fallen squarely on Lily's shoulders, and she was not going to give up until the Witch was on her way to Selsior.

Lily made her way towards the house to which the cats had run. As she approached the house, she saw a small vegetable garden around the side where she spotted tomatoes, potatoes, carrots, green beans and parsnips. Lily realised that the Witch must be living on a very simple diet – the animals on the farm were just there for the company, not for food! And she saw a herb garden there too, which Lily imagined the Witch kept for making her potions.

Out of nowhere, a black cat with a white streak bolted through the slightly ajar front door, which was then slammed shut once more. Lily approached the door and knocked on it gently. She looked down and saw that there was a pot of flowers on each side of the doorstep.

'Go away!' a voice inside shouted – a female voice.

'Please let me in, madam,' Lily said, surprised at the tone of the voice she had heard. 'I'm just here to talk to you. That's all I want to do. I just want to talk.'

'No, go away,' the voice said again.

'Please, I've come all this way,' Lily said. 'I want to talk to you about the Kingdom of Selsior. I want to talk about its plight.'

There was no answer this time, so Lily knocked on the door again, a bit more firmly. 'Hello?' she said. 'Hello!'

Lily stopped knocking and walked away from the door. But she was not giving up that easily. She walked around the side of the house without the vegetable garden and there was a window through which she could see a living room. There were a couple of tables, a few armchairs, a clock, a couple of paintings on the walls, piles of books, and a fireplace.

The first thing Lily saw, however, was a completely still black cat sat on a table right by the window, and it seemed to be looking outside the window. It still made no movement at all as Lily looked at it intently, even its eyes were not moving around. She realised it must be a very lifelike, life-sized sculpture of a cat. She looked at it even more closely, fascinated by the fact that the Witch, who had plenty of *real* cats, had decided to have a sculpture of a cat by her living room window. Lily's face was now so close to the window that she felt the coldness of the glass on her nose. Then one of the cat's front paws suddenly swiped the glass! It was a real cat after all, which had just been sitting very, very still. Lily screamed – it was a piercing scream, which she thought people might have heard back in Selsior.

Somebody entered the living room to see what the noise outside was. It was of course the Witch! Lily had finally caught sight of her. She was tall, with grey longish hair and sparkling blue eyes, which Lily could see even from quite far away. She did not have a long nose which Lily had been expecting, as *you* might have been expecting, and she had no warts to speak of either! The Witch was wearing a blue robe with a black belt and black short-heeled boots.

'I said, go away!' the Witch said firmly.

'I would just like to talk to you!' Lily repeated. 'Can we just have a chat? Please?'

The Witch sighed. 'Oh, fine!' she said in frustration. 'We can have a chat, you can tell me or ask me whatever it is you have to come to say or ask, and then you can go. All right?'

'All right,' Lily said, relieved. 'Thank you.' She smiled at the Witch, who turned and exited the living room.

The whistle of the kettle boiling on the Witch's kitchen stove was as piercing as Lily's scream had been just a few minutes before. Lily was sitting at the table in the middle of the kitchen, with her backpack on the floor by her feet.

The Witch poured some tea into two cups upon saucers and set the kettle back down on the stove. She then picked up a jug and poured some milk into the cups.

'Thank you very much,' Lily said. 'The last tea I drank was lukewarm!'

'In Selsior?' the Witch asked as she joined Lily at the table.

'No, in the Forest,' Lily said, 'on the journey here.'

'Oh, I see,' the Witch said. 'That must have been a long and difficult journey. It is a vast forest.'

'It is indeed,' Lily said, sipping the tea. 'Ooh, hot! Very hot!'

'Well, it's just boiled,' the Witch said drily.

'Yes, it has,' Lily said awkwardly.

'So instead of having an uncomfortable chat over a cup of tea, would you prefer to explain exactly why you are here?' the Witch asked.

'Yes, let's cut to the chase, shall we?' Lily said. 'Madam...'

'Please don't call me "madam",' the Witch interrupted.

'All right,' Lily said. 'So, as you may know, after the Magical Folk were banished from Selsior, the Goblins of the Forest invaded and conquered the Kingdom. The Goblins are cruel, vicious and violent, and they need to be kicked out of Selsior once and for all. So the people of the Kingdom sent five boys through the Forest to the Land of Zelnia, to come and speak to you, and to ask if you could help the people defeat the Goblins and reclaim our homeland... Oh, and I tagged along.'

'What happened to the five boys?' the Witch asked. 'Nothing terrible, I hope?'

'No, they decided to turn back at different stages of the journey,' Lily said. 'One of them, called Gregory, made it all the way here, but then chose to leave me to talk to you on my own.'

'And why was that?' the Witch asked.

'He thought it would just be better,' Lily replied.

'I see,' the Witch said bluntly. 'Well, um... Sorry, I have not even asked what your name is.'

'Lily,' Lily said.

'Well, Lily,' the Witch said, 'all I can say is that the people of Selsior got what was coming to them really – they sent away the Magical Folk who were protecting the Realm from the Goblins of the Forest, and then the Goblins attacked the Realm in the Magical Folk's absence. Now the people of Selsior want me, the last of the Magical Folk within a hundred miles, to come to their aid?'

'The King and Queen of Selsior have surely realised their mistake in banishing the Wizards and Witches from the Kingdom,' Lily said, 'and they would ask for the Magical Folk's forgiveness.'

'Do you know that?' the Witch asked. 'Do you know that they realised their mistake? Do you know that they would ask for forgiveness? Have you talked to them?'

'Well, not personally, but they would have realised that they'd made a serious mistake,' Lily said.

'Rulers make mistakes, and they pay the price for those mistakes,' the Witch said. 'The downfall of kingdoms and empires due to the arrogance and pride of their rulers has been a story told again and again, ever since the Unveiling of The World. Perhaps this is how the tale of Selsior was always supposed to end. It seems as inevitable as the changing of the seasons.'

'With all due respect, I don't think you really believe that,' Lily said.

'You are very persistent, aren't you, Lily?' the Witch asked, almost affectionately.

'I've been called stubborn in the past, yes,' Lily said. 'And I am stubbornly persisting because I have come through the Forest, and put myself in a lot of danger, to come and speak to you and ask for your help, for your *mercy*. And I have not come all this way to be rejected and turned away now.'

'Well, I am sorry to let you down, Lily,' the Witch said. 'But I do not see why *I* should help *your* people, when *they* were so unkind to *my* people.'

'But it was the King and Queen who were unkind to your people,' Lily countered. 'The people of Selsior are suffering horribly because of the King and Queen's decision to banish the Magical Folk.'

'I did not see the people of Selsior kicking up a fuss about our banishment,' the Witch said.

'There was nothing they could do!' Lily said, annoyed.

'Well, maybe there is nothing I can do now,' the Witch said. 'I mean, one Witch against the entire Goblin army? And the Empress? I do not like my chances...'

'But you've got magic on your side!' Lily said. 'You are much more powerful than the Goblins.'

'I am old now, Lily,' the Witch said. 'I am very old. I do not know if I would be powerful enough. I have lost much of the strength I used to possess.'

Lily dropped her head, feeling the accomplishment of her mission slipping further and further away from her. She never saw this part of the quest as the most difficult. She thought that once she had got through the dangerous Forest, and reached the Land of Zelnia, she would have basically completed the task – all she had to do was persuade the Witch to defeat the Goblins and free the

Kingdom of Selsior. But that persuasion had ended up being the hardest thing of all.

Lily was silent for a few moments, thinking. Then she asked the crucial question, the question that she had wanted to know the answer to ever since she discovered the Witch was alone in Zelnia: 'Why did you choose to stay in Zelnia all this time? Why didn't you move with your fellow Magical Folk to the Ancient Woodland in the West?'

The Witch sighed, then she answered: 'I want to live out the rest of my life in the same land as the ancestors whom I knew: my mother, my grandmother, and my great-grandmother. They were the women who I looked up to, respected and admired as I grew up and learnt the ways and traditions of the Magical Folk. The Enchanted Lands in the West do not have any great significance for me.'

'I understand that,' Lily said carefully. 'And I respect it. I do, honestly. But I think you stayed because you've also been waiting to be called back to the Kingdom of Selsior and save it.'

'All right then,' the Witch said resignedly. 'You are right, Lily. I was waiting to see if the people of Selsior were going to make contact with me. But the years passed and I heard nothing. Not a single whisper carried on the wind. The people's memory of me seemed to be lost, like a dream forgotten in the morning.'

'But *I* knew about you!' Lily said. '*I* wanted to come and talk to you.'

'It is too late now,' the Witch said. 'I will not help the people who were so unkind towards me and my people.'

'You are not the Witch I imagined when I was reading my book,' Lily said. 'That Witch would come and rescue the people of Selsior, despite what has happened in the past.'

'What book are you talking about?' the Witch asked.

Lily opened her backpack, got the book out, and placed it tenderly on the kitchen table. Lily noticed that the pages looked a bit more worn than when she had first taken it with her into the Forest.

'The History of the Kingdom of Selsior, the Forest, and the Land of Zelnia, from the 1st Era to the Present Day,' the Witch read out. 'You have read the whole book?'

'Yes, I have. Cover to cover!' Lily said. 'I love to read. I have lots and lots of books, but this is the biggest book I have ever read. It took me a while to read the whole thing.'

'I love to read too,' the Witch said. 'We have curiosity and a desire to learn in common, it seems.'

'I read about you in my book,' Lily said. 'About how you stayed here in Zelnia. I read about the different kinds of creatures in the Forest and how to talk to all of them. Everything I read, all of that information, helped me reach you. So please come and help my people. I beg you.'

'I am very sorry, Lily,' the Witch began, 'but your being so clever and curious is not enough for me to let go of the hurt your people caused me. The answer is "no", and that is my *final* answer.'

'So the journey has been in vain...' Lily said, heartbroken.

'I'm afraid so,' the Witch said.

Lily picked up her book and placed it in her backpack again. She buttoned the backpack and put it on her shoulders.

'Goodbye,' Lily said dejectedly.

'Goodbye,' the Witch said, then dropped her head.

Lily walked purposefully to the kitchen door. Then she stopped, turned round, and looked at the Witch. The Witch raised her head and saw Lily standing in the doorway.

'Before I go, there's something I want to say…' Lily began.

The Witch prepared herself for Lily to rant at her ferociously. Anger was often the last refuge of someone with no other options.

'I want to apologise to you and your kind,' Lily continued. 'Despite not being born at the time, let alone born into *royalty*, I am sorry for the way the Magical Folk were treated by the Kingdom of Selsior. After you had protected the Realm for decades, you were told to pack your bags and leave. It was cruel and unfair, and it was a huge injustice. They shouldn't have done it. So on behalf of the King and

Queen, and of all the people of Selsior, I am profoundly sorry. And I hope that you will forgive us someday.'

Lily then turned and walked out of the kitchen. She opened the front door, walked outside, and closed the door behind her.

Meanwhile in Selsior, a ginger-haired boy and a boy with hair so blonde it was almost white were sitting in a Goblin dungeon, both chained to the wall. Stephen was caught on the border between the Forest and Selsior, like Matthew, Jonathan and Timothy before him. Gregory had been chased by two Wolves from about halfway in the Forest. He thought that he might outrun the Wolves and make it back to Selsior to find his parents. The Wolves had bowled him over, then taken each of his feet in their jaws and dragged him to the castle under which the Goblins' prisoners were kept. He slightly regretted leaving Lily to talk to the Witch on her own.

They had not seen the three other boys since they had arrived, as they were in another cell somewhere. But at least they had each other, especially at that moment. Two Goblins had been assigned to question the two newest captives. They stood belligerently over Stephen and Gregory.

'Why were you in the Forest?' one of the Goblins asked them both.

Neither of the boys said anything. They looked at each other and silently agreed that they would not answer the Goblins' questions.

'Tell us why you were in the Forest!' the other Goblin said. 'What was your purpose? Who sent you into the Forest? Who or what were you trying to find?'

The boys stayed strong and continued to not give any answers. The Goblins grimaced and looked at each other. They were not in a patient sort of mood. Well, patience was not one of the Goblins' virtues anyway.

'We have methods of getting information out of prisoners, you know,' the first Goblin said. 'If you do not *willingly* tell us what you and your friends were up to, we will get the answers out of you *unwillingly*.'

'We are not going to tell you anything!' Gregory said. 'Willingly or unwillingly.'

'Fine,' the Goblin said. 'We will go and get the tools needed to persuade you to tell us everything we want to know.'

'Oh, you go and do that,' Gregory said cheekily.

'Watch your tongue,' the second Goblin said, 'or we might just remove it.'

'Well, that wouldn't help you get any information out of me, would it?' Gregory asked.

The Goblins exited the cell and shut the door behind them. Stephen turned to Gregory, puzzled.

'You're not the same boy I knew in the Forest, Gregory,' Stephen said. 'You've changed.'

'I got to know a very inspiring person on the journey,' Gregory said.

'Where is Lily?' Stephen asked. 'Is she safe?'

'Yes, Lily is safe,' Gregory said. 'And having a productive conversation with the Witch, I hope.'

Outside the cell, the two Goblins were discussing things.

'Are we really going to *interrogate* them?' the second Goblin asked.

'We will not need to,' the first Goblin said. 'The wait for us to come back will be the worst part of all. By the time we go into the cell again, they will have been dreading our return so much that they will want to spill everything.'

'Ah, I see,' the second Goblin said, smirking. 'Cunning.'

'Let's give them a few hours,' the first Goblin said, 'to agonise in anticipation...'

In Lily's home, Benjamin and Agatha thought all hope was lost. They had heard that all of the five boys who went into the Forest had been captured and put in the dungeons. Benjamin had to contend with two tragedies: the mission he had set in motion was over, and – more importantly – his eldest daughter was dead, somewhere out there in the midst of the Forest. Agatha had been inconsolable – she could not, and did not want to, imagine a life without Lily in it.

Edwin did not know what to think. He had not got his head around the idea that Lily could be gone forever. He missed her a lot, and made a promise to himself that if Lily did return, he would try to be a better brother.

Hilary, however, was one hundred per cent sure that Lily was alive. She was still really proud of her older sister; she wanted to be as brave as Lily when she was her age, and she felt confident that Lily would succeed in completing her task.

Far away in the Land of Zelnia, Lily held back her emotions as she set off towards the Forest. She now faced the journey home, a journey she was not expecting to make without the Witch by her side.

Chapter 11

RETURN

Lily approached the northern edge of the Forest. She reflected on her conversation with the Witch, and thought about any alternative approach she could have taken when asking the Witch for her help. Lily blamed herself for being too direct, too blunt about things. But after her mind filled with all the different possibilities, she concluded that she should not be too tough on herself. She had done the best she could in the circumstances.

Lily crossed the bridge over the river, and then set foot in the Forest. She thought of Gregory, with whom she had been when she was last in this part of the Forest. She hoped he was all right and that he would find his way home. With the memory of her time alone with Gregory, Lily burst into tears, never feeling so alone. She really wanted company for *this* journey, and Gregory was such great company.

Lily broke into a sprint, but as she started to feel the weight of her rucksack, she slowed down to a jog. She hoped that if she did not take any breaks in the journey, she would make it back to Selsior quickly. Soon enough, she would be home with her parents.

Lily knew that her parents would be incredibly angry, that they would lecture her about her disobedience from dawn to dusk for weeks on end, and that her father would most likely put iron bars outside her bedroom window to stop escaping. The window! Lily remembered that she had smashed the glass in her window to get out so she could go into the Forest. She would have to pay her parents back for fixing the damage with some of her pocket money, more of which she would probably never see.

Lily was so busy thinking about all these things that she was not looking where she was going. She did not see the tree root which was sticking out of the Forest floor. Lily's foot got caught in the root and she tripped – she went flying and hit the rough ground with quite a bump.

Ouch! Lily did not feel seriously hurt though, so she got up and dusted herself down. In the corner of her eye, she saw some movement. What was it? Lily nervously turned to her right, and she saw two of the Goblins' Wolves looking at her and snorting loudly. She did not scream, she did not even gasp, but ran as quickly as she could between the trees – running diagonally, as she thought that might help. It did not. The Wolves were hot on her trail.

But after a while of running, Lily looked behind her and did not see the Wolves chasing her anymore. She had escaped! She had no idea how – the Wolves were right behind her – but she had. She hid behind a tree and peeked around it to make sure that they were gone. They were. *Phew,* Lily thought, *that was a close shave!* There was silence in the Forest again and Lily felt safe now. A gentle breeze blew across her face and it felt soothing and refreshing.

Lily moved away from the tree trunk and found herself face-to-face with one of the Wolves.

She did gasp this time. She turned the other way and the second Wolf was behind her.

There was no way out, Lily thought. This was the end. This was how she was going to die. Not as an old woman in many decades' time, in a free Selsior, with her own family at her bedside, but eaten by Wolves in the Forest. Or maybe they would just take hold of her and escort to the Goblins? Perhaps she could still escape somewhere on the journey, or when she was in Selsior. Perhaps she still had a chance of survival. All of these thoughts were interrupted by the low snarling of the Wolves. Both of their mouths opened wide, revealing their razor-sharp teeth, then...

The Wolves were suddenly stopped! Lily heard a voice say something in a mysterious language, and a shape resembling a bubble, full of light, exploded in between the two Wolves. They were knocked sideways, unconscious, like the Giants had done earlier, but in an even more powerful and effective way.

Lily looked at the two Wolves lying there, then turned to see the person behind her deliverance from them. It was as Lily had hoped as soon as she heard the voice: the Witch had come to save her! She must have cast some kind of spell to knock out the Wolves. Lily smiled at the Witch, beaming with relief and with happiness. She saw that the Witch was now wearing a long blue cloak, and carrying a purple wand and a broomstick.

'Does this mean you are coming to rescue Selsior?' Lily asked.

'Yes, I will come with you to help your people take back your kingdom,' the Witch answered.

'That is fantastic!' Lily said, hugging the Witch, who put her arm around Lily. 'What changed your mind?'

'It's not a matter of *what* changed my mind,' the Witch said, 'but *who* changed my mind.'

'You're going to overthrow the Goblins and reinstate the King and Queen?' Lily asked.

'Yes, I am,' the Witch said. 'And I shan't be doing it alone.'

'What do you mean, me?' Lily asked. 'I can't help beat the Goblin army!'

'No, you can't do this part, Lily,' the Witch, 'but I know others who *can* help me...'

Lily looked at the Witch confused. The Witch then raised her wand in the air and cast a bright spell into the sky, which then seemed to descend on the Forest like rainfall.

'What was that?' Lily asked.

'It was a signal to rally the troops!' the Witch said excitedly. 'The creatures of the Forest – Giants, Gnomes, Bats and Fairies.'

'They're going to help defeat the Goblins?' Lily asked.

'Yes,' the Witch said. 'They will be a force to reckon with, will they not?' She released her broomstick, which then hovered in the air, and she climbed upon it. She looked at Lily. 'Come aboard, Lily! You need a ride back home!'

'You're kidding!' Lily said.

'Do I look like I'm kidding?' the Witch responded, smiling.

'This is brilliant,' Lily said, brimming with glee. 'This is absolutely brilliant.'

Lily climbed upon the broomstick behind the Witch and held on tightly.

'Are you ready?' the Witch asked.

'Yes!' Lily said jubilantly.

Whoosh! The broomstick shot off with huge momentum, scattering dust and dirt from the Forest floor. The Witch and Lily flew through the Forest at great speed, even faster than Lily's flight on the back of the Bat the previous day, and this was even more thrilling!

As they went through the different territories of the Forest, the creatures from each territory joined the Witch in her journey to Selsior, headed up by their leaders: the Lord of the Giants, the King of the Gnomes, the Master of the Bats (which was especially remarkable because the Bats were nocturnal), and the Queen of the Fairies. They were certainly a force to be reckoned with.

Before Lily knew it, she and the Witch were in the Kingdom of Selsior. Lily thought about how quickly the journey back to Selsior had been compared to the journey to Zelnia!

The Witch stopped her broomstick. 'This is where I must leave you, Lily,' she said. 'I am going to go and find the Empress. I will look for you after the battle is over.'

Lily got off the broomstick. 'Thank you for the ride home,' she said. 'I will see you later! Good luck!'

The Witch zoomed off again. Then Lily was surrounded by the army of the Fairies, the Bats, the Gnomes and the Giants. But they all ran and flew past her.

The creatures of the Forest charged into the roads and streets, into the marketplace, and into every other part of the Kingdom of Selsior, far and wide. They captured every Goblin they found, and they bound them all together with rope.

The Goblins realised they were under attack by the creatures of the Forest. They had never expected that. They expected the people of Selsior to rise up against them and fight them, but they did not in their wildest dreams think that the different creatures in the Forest would unite to take them on.

The Goblins were completely and utterly unprepared! They scrambled together as many of them as they could, and formed lines and lines in front of the Palace of the Empress.

The army of Fairies, Bats, Gnomes and Giants were joined by the people of Selsior, both men and women, who were inspired by the creatures sweeping through the Kingdom and overwhelming the Goblins. This army formed lines and lines too, in opposition to their Goblin adversaries. The people were armed with sticks and rocks, as they did not have any other weapons to wield.

'Charge!' the Lord of the Giants roared.

At the Lord of the Giants' command, the army of the creatures of the Forest and the people of Selsior advanced with great speed towards the Goblin army. The Goblins, rather reluctantly, started to run in the direction of the incoming tide of creatures and people. Battle cries from both sides filled the air. The two armies soon met in the middle and began to fight. The battle for the future of Selsior had commenced.

Lily ran to her house and knocked on the door. Benjamin opened the door. His eyes widened in disbelief – Lily was back! She was alive! Benjamin embraced Lily tightly.

'Lily, I am so happy to see you!' he said. 'How *are* you?'

'I am so happy to see you too, Dad!' Lily said. 'And I am all right!'

'Lily?' someone said behind Benjamin. It was Agatha. She saw her eldest daughter and burst into tears. 'Lily!'

Benjamin let go of Lily and Agatha gave her a big hug.

'Oh, my goodness, Lily,' Agatha said, 'I never thought I'd see you again...'

'I am so sorry for sneaking out,' Lily said, withdrawing from her mother's arms, 'and for smashing the glass in my bedroom window.'

'That's all in the past now,' Agatha said. 'We're both just happy that you're back safe and well.'

'And the mission is accomplished!' Lily said. 'The Witch has come to help get rid of the Goblins.

And an army of the creatures of the Forest and the people of Selsior are fighting the Goblin army in battle.'

'She has? They are?' Benjamin asked in disbelief.

'Yes and yes!' Lily answered.

'Oh, Lily, you did so well!' Agatha exclaimed. 'I'm so proud of you. I'm sorry I ever doubted you.'

'Yes, me too,' Benjamin said proudly, 'but I'd better go now – I should be in the battle.'

'No, please don't go,' Lily said. 'Please, Dad!'

'Lily, you have played your massive part in reclaiming the Kingdom of Selsior,' Benjamin said proudly. 'Now I must go and play my small part in it.'

'Just come back alive,' Agatha said, before kissing her husband. Benjamin then ran in the direction of the Palace, where the conflict was taking place.

'Come in now, Lily, come in,' Agatha said.

Agatha put an arm around Lily to take her into the house, but Lily stood firmly still.

'We need to release Uncle Simon from the Goblin dungeons!' Lily said. 'And all the prisoners who have been locked up in them.'

'Oh, and the five boys who went into the Forest!' Agatha said.

'Were they all captured?' Lily asked agitatedly.

'Yes, they were,' Agatha said.

'Let's go!' Lily said.

'Wait,' Agatha said. 'Edwin! Hilary!'

Edwin and Hilary both ran out of the living room inside. They had not heard Lily come back.

'Lily!' Edwin yelled.

'Lily, you're back!' Hilary said joyfully.

'Yes, I am back now,' Lily said. 'But we can catch up later – we are going to release the prisoners from the Goblin dungeons!'

'Hooray!' Edwin and Hilary both said enthusiastically.

'So let's go!' Lily said. She went to move, then felt the weight of her rucksack on her shoulders. She took the rucksack off and placed it down on the floor in her house. It was such a relief not to be carrying such a heavy load on her back!

Agatha closed the door behind her children, then they all ran off towards the castle together.

The Witch flew to the Palace of the Empress, outside which the great battle was being fought. She cast spells at all of the Goblins she encountered on the way. She flew above the archway and blasted open the drawbridge of the Palace, full of daggers pointing outwards. She made it past all of the Goblin guards and told all of the human servants that they were free. She flew through the corridors of the Palace looking for the right room, and she soon found it: the Throne Room. She got off her broomstick.

The Witch cast a spell to break the lock on the door to the Throne Room and walked inside. Her Imperial Majesty, the Empress of the Goblins was sat on her throne, wearing her golden armour and black jagged crown, and holding her dark green sceptre. She looked grief-stricken, heartbroken, but still mighty and powerful in her full regalia.

The Witch stood silently observing the Empress for a few tense moments, as the Goblin leader had not looked up to see the intruder yet. Eventually, the Empress raised her head and beheld the Witch in the doorway of her Throne Room. *How dare she come here uninvited and unannounced?* the Empress thought.

'I knew this day would come,' the Empress of the Goblins said. 'You have come to assassinate me. I warned my generals that the people of Selsior were going to beg you to help them, like the pathetic creatures they are...'

'Your Reign is over, Empress,' the Witch said. 'The people of Selsior are taking their kingdom back.'

'No, you are taking their kingdom back for them!' the Empress said, before jumping out of her throne to attack the Witch.

The Witch pre-empted the Empress' move and cast a spell. The Empress instantly raised her sceptre and the spell bounced off it. The Witch cast spell after spell, and the Empress deflected every single one.

There were now two battles going on in the Kingdom. There was the battle between two armies being fought *outside* the Palace, and there was the one-on-one battle being fought *inside* the Palace. The destiny of Selsior hung in the balance until both of those battles were over.

Lily led Agatha, Edwin and Hilary into the castle where the Goblins' prisoners were being kept. Lily hoped that her uncle and the five boys with whom she had gone into the Forest were all alive and well.

All the doors had been left open because of the rush the Goblins had been in to gather an army together, which was very fortunate for these intrepid liberators! The group entered the castle, and Edwin saw steps going down somewhere to the right.

They descended the steps and they found themselves in a long and wide corridor full of prison cells, which went round a corner. They could not tell how many cells in total there were.

Agatha held Edwin and Hilary's hands very tightly as they entered. Lily gasped as she saw a Troll sitting down on a stool at the opposite end of the corridor. In one hand the Troll was holding a bunch of keys; in the other hand it was holding a club.

'Troll!' Edwin said a bit too loudly.

'Shush, Edwin!' Agatha said with a smile.

Lily turned to Agatha. 'I'm going to get the Troll's keys,' she said.

'We'll create a diversion,' Agatha said.

'Good idea,' Lily said, before running to hide in one of the prison cell doorways, where the Troll could not see her.

'What's a diversion, Mum?' Hilary asked.

'It's another word for a distraction, Hilary,' Agatha said. 'It's when you distract somebody.'

'Oh, I see,' Hilary said.

What this distraction was going to be, Agatha had no idea yet. But Hilary thought for a few moments, then inspiration struck.

'I know how we can distract them,' Hilary said.

Agatha listened to Hilary's plan. And it was a very good one! So they went about carrying it out.

Agatha, Edwin and Hilary walked slowly towards the Troll, which still had its back to them all.

Hilary then got a small flute out of her cardigan pocket.

Hilary had always carried her flute around with her because she loved to play it whenever the mood took her – when she was happy, when she was sad, when she was excited about something, when she was bored of something – and she often played for her family, ever since Benjamin and Agatha realised that she had a talent for it.

Hilary played a soothing tune on her flute and the Troll started looking sleepy very quickly. She played the tune for a minute or so, and the Troll slumped and its head was properly drooping.

Agatha joined Hilary's tune by singing a lullaby over it, with the words she had used to send each of her three children off to sleep when they were younger: 'Close your eyes, go to sleep, your day is now done. Close your eyes, go to sleep, till the rising of the sun.'

Edwin wanted to be included, so he hummed along to Hilary's tune and his mother's song.

The Troll began to snore very loudly. It was asleep! Hilary's plan had worked. Hilary stopped playing and put the flute back into her cardigan pocket. Lily, meanwhile, walked gingerly towards the Troll and slipped the bunch of keys out of its hand. She held them aloft, then ran back to Agatha, Edwin and Hilary.

'That was brilliant!' Lily said. 'Well done, Mum!'

'Oh, no, it wasn't my idea,' Agatha said, 'it was Hilary's idea.'

'Well done, Hilary, then!' Lily said. 'Right, I'd better release the prisoners...'

One by one, Lily unlocked each prison cell. The prisoners came out thanking Lily and hugging her. She told them not to speak too loudly so they would not rouse the Troll. After quietly thanking Lily, they all walked up the steps to freedom.

Eventually, Lily found the captives to whom she was particularly attached: her uncle Simon, then the five boys – Matthew, Jonathan, Timothy, Stephen and Gregory.

Simon embraced Lily, then Agatha, Edwin and Hilary. Agatha told him all about what Lily had done, and that the people of Selsior were fighting a great battle against the Goblins alongside the creatures of the Forest. Simon was amazed, then he apologised to Lily for not listening properly to her advice about making contact with the Witch in the Land of Zelnia. Lily said that was all in the past; their focus now should be on the present, and the future.

Then the five boys formed a circle around Lily and they closed in to have a group hug with her.

'Boys! Boys!' Lily said, beginning to suffocate. 'All right, all right!' She turned to her family members. 'Mum, Edwin, Hilary, Uncle Simon, these boys here are called Matthew, Jonathan, Timothy, Stephen and Gregory. They were on the journey into the Forest when I crashed the party. They very graciously let me join them.'

'And Lily very quickly became the leader!' Matthew said.

'Lily helped us go further and further through the Forest,' Stephen said. 'Before I turned back.'

'She talked to the creatures!' Gregory said. 'And she made it to the other side, in the Land of Zelnia.'

'It seems like you have quite the fan club, Lily,' Agatha said.

'And we are sorry for leaving you,' Jonathan said.

'Yes, and for abandoning the mission,' Timothy said.

'Don't apologise, don't be sorry,' Lily said. 'You all did well in your own way. Most importantly, you were all there when I needed you. And it is all right to be afraid, we are all afraid at one time or another, because feeling fear does not mean that you're a coward, but that you've realised your limitations.'

'You always know the right thing to say!' Gregory said.

'Yes, that was a very kind and wise thing to say, Lily,' Uncle Simon said.

'She gets it from her mum,' Agatha said, smiling.

'Of course,' Lily said, then paused for a moment. 'I also read a lot!'

'We shouldn't stand around chin-wagging though,' Uncle Simon said. 'Let's go and see how the battle is going.'

After Lily had placed the bunch of keys upon a hook on the wall of the corridor, the whole group ran to the steps and ascended them.

The group ran towards the Palace and they saw that the Goblins were running away from the battle.

'Retreat! Retreat!' the Goblins yelled as they ran to the Palace, knowing that all was lost.

'Victory! Liberty!' the people of Selsior declared. 'Victory and liberty! The Goblins are defeated!'

Lily's family members looked around for Benjamin. After a few moments of desperately searching for him, there he was! He saw his brother, wife, and children and ran over to them, embracing each of them.

'The battle is won,' Benjamin said. 'The Goblins have been pushed back. What of the King and Queen, and the Prince?'

'The King and Queen!' Lily exclaimed. She had been so focused on releasing her uncle and the five boys that she had almost forgotten about the former rulers. 'But we opened all of the prison cells in the castle.'

'Perhaps they were put in another castle in the Kingdom?' Agatha said.

'Why would the Goblins separate them?' Benjamin asked.

'What if they are not in a castle?' Lily said.

'What do you mean?' Agatha asked.

'I read in my book that when the King and Queen were in power, people who were arrested for treason and sentenced to execution were actually put in a special dungeon underneath the Palace,' Lily said. 'And the King and Queen would look at the traitor, or traitors, through a small hole in the ceiling of the dungeon. What if the Empress of the Goblins knew about that special dungeon and imprisoned the King and Queen in there? And took pleasure in looking at them through the hole?'

'That sounds like something the Goblins and their wicked Empress would do,' Benjamin said.

'Let's go to the Palace to find the special dungeon and release the King and Queen,' Lily said.

'All right,' Benjamin said. 'Let's go.'

Lily's family members and the five boys all ran towards the Palace, unaware that a great battle was still being fought within its walls. The only thing they were thinking about was freeing the King and Queen of the Realm, so their rule could be restored, while the Reign of the Goblins would finally come to an end.

In the Throne Room of the Empress of the Goblins, the Witch was still casting spells at the Empress, which were being deflected again and again. The Witch could not find a way to overcome the Empress. She was using every spell she could remember, but her memory was fading due to her old age, and she could not recall the one she needed to break through. Meanwhile, the Empress could not get any closer to strike the Witch, because of all the many spells being fired in her direction.

'You know you are pathetic too, don't you, *Witch*?' the Empress said tauntingly. 'You are being used by the deceitful people of Selsior to fight their battles for them! You have become their servant! Their maid! Coming to clean up the mess that they created... all because of their arrogance and pride.' The Empress had strangely echoed a phrase the Witch had used when speaking to Lily earlier that day.

But the Witch thought differently now: 'It was my choice to help the people of Selsior take back their kingdom,' she said. 'The World does not need to put up with cruel and greedy bullies like the Goblins. So I am here to put an end to your rule over this land once and for all.'

'I will see this Palace razed to the ground and the whole Kingdom of Selsior reduced to rubble before I ever relinquish power!' the Empress shouted.

'There is no point trying to cling onto that which has already been lost,' the Witch said.

Then the Witch remembered something, something in the very back of her mind, something which she had learnt at school many, many years ago, but she had been taught to use it only in extreme circumstances. She felt that her current situation qualified.

With a flick of her wrist and the right series of words, the Witch cast a huge spell at the Empress which knocked the sceptre out of her hand and the crown off her head.

'No!' the Empress shrieked. 'You can't do this!'

'I just did,' the Witch said.

The Witch cast another spell, a spell which summoned the sceptre from the corner of the room and twisted it around the Empress' wrists in such a way that it created handcuffs. The Witch cast one more spell which made the metal of the sceptre strong enough to restrain the Empress indefinitely.

'Let me go!' the Empress screamed. 'Let me go!'

The Witch did not let the Empress go, obviously. What she did instead was to place the Empress on the back of her broomstick. The Witch then climbed on the front of the broomstick and flew out of the

Throne Room. They flew through the corridors, down the steps, and out of the Palace.

The Witch then flew quickly to the castle. The people who saw the Empress on the back of the Witch's broomstick cheered as they saw that the leader of the Goblins had been defeated and placed under arrest. She was now completely powerless.

The Empress was put into the prison in the bowels of the castle, where the Fairies, the Bats, the Gnomes and the Giants had been putting the Goblin captives, as well as any Goblin survivors of the great battle, for the last hour or so.

'I will have my revenge!' the Empress of the Goblins screamed. 'You mark my words! I will have my revenge!'

The Witch slammed the Empress' cell door shut and locked it, using the bunch of keys that Lily had left upon the hook on the wall. She did the same with all of the doors in the long corridor.

After she was done, the Witch handed the bunch of keys to the Troll, who had been woken up by the Witch when she arrived. Instead of just holding the keys, the Troll held them high above its head, tilted its head back, opened its mouth, and dropped the keys into its mouth! There was a loud *gulp* as the Troll swallowed the keys. The Witch was completely taken aback, but understood what the Troll meant by the gesture: the Goblins were *never* getting out.

'Guard them anyway!' the Witch said chirpily.

The Troll nodded, and half-smiled. It was a strange sight for the Witch to witness...

The Witch left the castle and flew back towards the Palace. While she had been flying around the Palace searching for the Empress of the Goblins, the Witch had sensed that the King and Queen and the Prince were being held there somewhere – she had seen their faces and felt their presence very close by.

But on her way back, the Witch saw a lot of bodies lying on the ground in the aftermath of the great battle that had been fought outside the Palace. Some of the fighters – humans, Fairies, Bats, Gnomes, Giants – were dead, but the majority were injured and in need of urgent care.

The Witch walked to the first body she came across and got out a small jar from her cloak pocket. You see, the Witch had thought ahead when she set off from her home in Zelnia – she had brought a jar of healing potion with her. She set about healing the wounds of the people and creatures surrounding her.

And this was not the only healing that the Witch would be providing that day. She knew that the Kingdom of Selsior had been rescued; now it needed to be restored and repaired.

Chapter 12

FREEDOM

In the special dungeon beneath the Palace of Selsior, there were three people sitting on the floor: a man, a woman, and a boy.

The man was in his mid-forties, handsome, black-haired with traces of silver on each side of his head, and he had brown eyes. The woman was in her late thirties, very beautiful, with long and wavy blonde hair, blue eyes, and a small mole on her left cheek. The boy was in his mid-teens, with brown hair and brown eyes, and he had his father's good looks.

These three people made up the royal family of Selsior, who had been locked up in this special dungeon for the last twelve years. The King and Queen had been seized by the Goblins and placed in this dungeon while they were wearing all of their royal clothing and finery. In the corner of the room, there was a pile of purple robes, bejewelled silver rings and golden crowns. The Prince had not known a life outside these four walls, as he had been put in the dungeon with his parents as a toddler.

The King and Queen never thought their imprisonment would last this long – they believed that the Goblins would be ousted and Selsior reclaimed fairly soon after their invasion. But their optimism and hope soon turned to desolation and despair, as the days and weeks turned into months and years. They were only aware that a new day had begun when they heard the sound of a Troll guard arriving above and dropping a loaf of bread and a bottle of water through the hole in the ceiling. They knew the provision of food and drink by the Goblins was cruelty rather than charity – the longer the King and Queen were kept alive, the longer they suffered the humiliation of being deposed and imprisoned.

During their time in captivity, the former King of Selsior thought a lot about his heritage and his royal ancestors. He had learnt about the history of the Kingdom when he was a young prince being educated by his tutors.

The King's grandfather had challenged the corrupt and bloodthirsty tyrant called the Iron-handed King for the throne. His grandfather met the tyrant in battle and defeated him, and he took the crown from his head. He became known as the Heroic King, who saved the Kingdom of Selsior from a madman. As you are beginning to see, the Kings of Selsior were known by the nicknames they were given.

The Heroic King died and passed the crown to the oldest of his three sons, and this son became a very good king indeed. He was the King who invited the Magical Folk to live in Selsior and share in its plenty, in return for their protection over the Kingdom. This King was once described as "the embodiment of morality", so he became the Moral King.

The Moral King passed away and his only son inherited the throne of Selsior. It was this king who made the unwise decision to ban magic across the Kingdom and banish the Magical Folk. The King knew that he had made a catastrophic mistake, one he desperately wished he could erase. He also knew that he was a deeply flawed man, and he feared that he was doomed to go down in history as the Foolish King, or the Reckless King, or the *Disastrous* King. When he was very hungry, or very thirsty, he began to hallucinate that his father and grandfather were visiting him in the dungeon to express their disappointment in him.

What the King did not know was that outside the Palace, across Selsior, there had been debates among the people about what right the King had to sit on the throne again, if the Goblins were ever defeated. There was some speculation that the King would be replaced by one of the ambitious men of the Kingdom in some kind of election, but it was eventually decided that Selsior would need some stability after its liberation from the Goblins.

The King was still thinking about how he would be known after he died when he heard voices approaching above. He looked up, as did the Queen and the Prince, at the moment a girl's face appeared through the hole in the ceiling.

'Hello, Your Majesties!' the girl said.

The royal family all stood up, mouths agape at the sight of people up above. People! Not the Empress of the Goblins coming to taunt and tease them again.

'Mama, what's happening?' the Prince asked timidly.

'I don't know, sweetheart,' the Queen said.

'Who are you?' the King asked. 'What's going on?'

'My name is Lily,' Lily said. 'Selsior is free! The Goblins have been defeated!'

'And the Empress of the Goblins!' another voice said.

Lily turned around, and behind her parents, her siblings, her uncle, and the five boys, she saw the Witch approaching.

'The Empress has been defeated?' Lily asked.

'Yes, and locked up in the castle dungeon with the rest of the Goblins,' the Witch said. 'And the Troll guard swallowed the keys!'

Everyone laughed and cheered. Then they remembered that they still had to release the King and Queen and the Prince from their imprisonment.

'How do we find the entrance to the dungeon?' Lily asked.

The King of Selsior gave long and complicated directions as to where the dungeon was located in the Palace. The group set off, and between them they remembered the King's directions as they went along.

The group reached a black door. The Witch looked for a lock, but there was none to be found.

'How do we get inside?' Lily asked.

'The door has been *sealed* shut,' the Witch said.

'Oh, goodness,' Agatha said. 'How are we going to get the King and Queen out?'

The Witch produced her wand from her cloak pocket and showed it to Agatha, smiling.

'Ah, of course!' Agatha said, smiling back.

The Witch cast a spell at the door which soon unsealed it. 'Stand away from the door!' the Witch told the royal family. After a few moments, she pushed the door and it fell down onto the ground, revealing behind it the King, the Queen and the Prince.

The royal family ran to the doorway and thanked the Witch, Lily, Lily's family members, and the five boys.

'You are our rescuers!' the King said tearfully.

'The Reign of the Goblins is over,' the Witch said. 'Your reign will now resume. You must rule well, Your Majesties, and observe honour, justice and peace in everything you do.'

'We will!' the Queen exclaimed.

'Yes, we promise we will,' the King said.

'I am certain of it,' the Witch said warmly.

'And we ask for your forgiveness,' the King said, 'for the way we banished the Magical Folk. Can you find it in your heart to forgive us?'

'Oh, yes,' the Witch said. 'All is forgiven and forgotten... Though the last part may be because I am very old!'

Lily laughed.

'Why did you come back?' the Queen asked. 'Why did you come to help get rid of the Goblins and free us from prison?'

The Witch chuckled. 'Hmm... Why did I not let you continue in your suffering?' she asked rhetorically. 'Why did I choose to save you and help your people, even though you banished the Magical Folk from Selsior after we had protected you for all those years? Well, in this case, I found that all of the harshness and ingratitude of a whole kingdom can be outweighed by the courage and kindness of one girl.'

After she said this, the Witch moved to the side to let the King and Queen see Lily, who was stood at the front of the group as her family and the five boys had stepped backwards.

'This one girl?' the King asked. 'Well, *thank you*! And what is your name, child?'

'Lily,' Lily said.

'Would it be all right if the Queen and I hugged you?' the King asked.

'Yes, that would be all right with me!' Lily said.

The King and Queen both embraced Lily tightly. Lily knew for certain now that she had achieved all that she had set out to achieve.

On the way out of the Palace, the Witch explained the whole story: how it was Lily's idea to go through the Forest to the Land of Zelnia on the other side, in order to ask the Witch for her help; how the five boys had gone into the Forest and Lily had joined them; how the five boys had each chosen to return to Selsior and left Lily to speak to the Witch alone; and how Lily had apologised to the Witch on the King and Queen's behalf, causing the Witch to choose to rescue the Kingdom. The King and Queen listened in astonishment and wonder at all that Lily had done.

Chapter 13

PEACE AND HARMONY

The Witch led the King and Queen, the Prince, Lily, Lily's family, and the five boys to the Great Hall, in the east of the Kingdom. The Witch had told town-criers to announce to the whole population of Selsior that a very important event was taking place in the Great Hall, and they were all invited inside and outside the hall to be a part of it.

The Witch cast a spell which completely transformed the Great Hall from the deteriorating building it had been for so long into a grand, magnificent place again. Then the guests started to arrive, the people of Selsior, the Fairies, the Bats, the Gnomes and the Giants. The Queen of the Fairies, the Master of the Bats, the King of the Gnomes and the Lord of the Giants were at the front of the hall –

hovering, hanging from a chandelier, or simply standing.

The very important event began. The King and Queen processed from the back of the Great Hall to the front, where the Witch was waiting. Before they left the Palace, the King and Queen had put their robes and their rings back on, but the Witch had held onto their crowns. So when the King and Queen reached the front of the hall, the Witch placed the correct crown on each of their heads.

'The King and Queen of Selsior have been crowned once more!' the Witch proclaimed, to cheering and whooping from the crowds gathered. 'They have promised to rule well, and to observe honour, justice and peace in everything they do. And in many, many years' time, Your Majesty, after you are gone, you will be known evermore as the *Redeemed* King.'

The King bowed his head to the Witch, who bowed her head in return. They then turned to watch the Prince processing from the back of the hall to the front. He was still getting used to life outside the dungeon, let alone adjusting to his role as the heir to the throne of Selsior.

The Witch placed a third crown on his head. The crowds cheered and whooped again, especially some girls towards the front who found this young prince very attractive.

The Witch then moved to the side so the royal family were on display to everyone in the Great Hall. The King and Queen held hands, and the Queen put her arm around the Prince. There was a round of applause at the sight of the royal family. The King gestured for the crowd to quieten.

'We very much appreciate your applause,' the King said, 'but we are not deserving of it. And I want to apologise for my mistake, my serious error of judgement, when I banned magic and banished the Wizards and Witches from Selsior. I am sorry that I allowed the Goblins to invade and conquer this kingdom, and that you have suffered for all of these years. I ask for your forgiveness, and I hope you can all accept my retaking of the throne.'

'We forgive you!' one man shouted, leading the way for all the people shouting words of approval and forgiveness.

'I am humbled and deeply honoured by your kindness,' the King said.

'We both are,' the Queen said, holding her husband's hand tightly. 'We will devote all of our time and energy to rebuilding Selsior now. And we will use the riches of this Kingdom to do so. Instead of hoarding the gold in the Palace as we did before, we will use it and share it around.'

There was another round of applause. The people had never heard such generosity from their rulers before.

'But we are not the heroes of this tale, by any stretch of the imagination,' the King said. 'No, somebody else here is the true hero, or heroine, and we want to thank her publicly. Lily, where are you?'

A very embarrassed and blushing Lily showed herself, sheepishly raising her hand.

'Can you come up here, Lily?' the King asked.

Lily walked up to the front and stood between the Witch and the royal family, feeling very self-conscious in front of this massive crowd.

'Lily was the person who suggested the idea of going through the Forest to the Land of Zelnia to ask the Witch for her help in defeating the Goblins,' the King said.

The crowd burst into applause, and Matthew, Jonathan, Timothy, Stephen and Gregory cheered and whooped *very* loudly.

'So we thank the Witch for coming to save the Kingdom of Selsior,' the King said. He then turned to speak to the Witch directly: 'And the Queen and I would like you to know that you are welcome to stay in Selsior for as long as you want!'

The Witch smiled and bowed her head.

'And we thank Lily for bravely going on the journey through the Forest to find the Witch,' the King continued.

'There are others who should be thanked for the parts they played, Your Majesty,' Lily said. 'I would like to thank Matthew, Jonathan, Timothy, Stephen and Gregory for being there on the journey with me. Each of you was with me for different lengths of time, but nonetheless, you were all there!'

The five boys looked at each other laughing, flanked by their families, who were all very proud of their sons.

'I would also like to thank the Queen of the Fairies, the Master of the Bats, the King of the Gnomes, and the Lord of the Giants,' Lily said, 'firstly for letting us pass through the Forest, and secondly for leading their kinds into battle against the Goblins alongside the people of Selsior.'

The leaders of the four kinds of creatures all bowed their heads, although the Master of the Bats actually raised his head because he was upside down.

Lily continued: 'And the fundamental lesson we can learn from everything that has happened in the past is this: if all of us – the people of Selsior and the creatures of the Forest – can just tolerate and accept each other, we can all live in peace and harmony. And that is all that matters in the end.'

There were mutters of agreement among the crowd and a general nodding of heads. Such insight from such a young person!

'We agree completely, Lily,' the King said. 'You are a very wise girl, and we are very fortunate to have you in our Kingdom.'

'And we have a proposition for you personally,' the Queen said. 'As the rulers of the Realm, we need to think about its future, and about who will be ruling it once we are gone. So, Lily, we propose that you wed the Prince when you are both of marrying age. You will become the Princess of Selsior, and someday you will be Queen... How does that sound to you?'

Lily was stunned, flabbergasted, and speechless! She had never expected such a proposal, especially here in front of all these people. She tried to collect her thoughts so she could answer lucidly and courteously.

'Thank you for the offer, Your Majesties,' Lily began, 'but I will have to say "no".'

There was an audible gasp from the girls swooning over the Prince at the front of the hall.

'Please don't get me wrong,' Lily continued. 'The Prince is very handsome, and I am sure he is a lovely young man. But now that the Goblins have been defeated and Selsior has been recovered, I wish to have a very ordinary life! I am not seeking any prestige for myself, or even any high status. So I must respectfully decline.'

The King and Queen both bowed their heads and smiled, fully understanding Lily's reasoning. The Prince, meanwhile, did not react at all – who knew what *he* had thought about the whole idea!

'And we respectfully accept your respectful decline,' the Queen said.

'But we have *another* offer for you,' the King said. 'An offer of a title. We wish to give you the title of the Peacekeeper of Selsior. We will ask you for your guidance and counsel regarding the conduct of the Realm. If you are willing?'

'Yes, I am willing to fill that role!' Lily said with a grin.

'Superb,' the King said, smiling back. The title was officially bestowed upon Lily there and then.

The ceremony was then over. The King and Queen and the Prince processed from the front of the Great Hall to the back, then outside, where there were crowds lining the long road to the Palace. The King, Queen and Prince turned left and walked in the direction of the Palace.

The Witch followed the royal family outside. Seeing that the Palace in the distance was still looking horrible from when the Empress of the Goblins had given it a makeover, the Witch fired a spell which flew through the air, and seemed to explode over the Palace.

The Palace changed before the King and Queen's very eyes: the King and Queen's banners and flags reappeared in their places; the outer wall and the keep were a cream colour like they were before; the original drawbridge was restored; and the green and gloopy slime in the moat became water again. The transformation was a joyous and beautiful sight to behold.

The King and Queen thanked the Witch for her renovation of their home, before they disappeared from her sight behind the crowds, which came together from the sides of the road to follow the royal family as they strode to the Palace.

Meanwhile, the Queen of the Fairies, the Master of the Bats, the King of the Gnomes, and the Lord of the Giants, led their respective kinds back into the Forest, in the knowledge that they would all be enjoying friendly and considerate relationships with the Kingdom of Selsior from that point onwards. Lily said goodbye to each of the leaders as they left the Great Hall.

The people of Selsior who had attended the ceremony were the next to exit the Great Hall, and they quickly dispersed. Lily and her family walked out of the hall, discussing the title that had been given to Lily: the Peacekeeper of Selsior! What a wonderful thing to be for the Kingdom.

Matthew, Jonathan, Timothy, Stephen and Gregory searched for Lily. They found her and ran to her, hugging her and congratulating her on her new role in the Kingdom. They joked about how they were all famous now, and how they would be recognised everywhere they went. The five boys then said goodbye, for the time being, and waved as they walked back to their families and went home.

The Witch then approached Lily. 'May we go for a walk together, Lily?' she asked.

'Yes, just give me a second,' Lily said. She turned to her parents: 'Is it all right if I meet you at home in a little while?'

'Yes, of course,' Benjamin and Agatha said. 'We'll see you in a bit.'

The Witch and Lily then separated from Lily's family and began walking north. Benjamin held Hilary's hand and Agatha held Edwin's hand as they set off home together.

Chapter 14

JOURNEY'S END

The Witch and Lily chatted about all kinds of things as they walked north with each other. Firstly, they just discussed the weather (it was a bright and rather mild sunny day), but then they got to more personal matters: Lily's family; the Witch's family; the Witch's experience of life among the Magical Folk in the Land of Zelnia, and then her time on her own; and everything about Lily's journey through the Forest. Lily felt that it was the conversation of two people who only had a very short amount of time to get to know one another.

Lily had not been paying much attention to where they were walking – the Witch had been leading their seemingly leisurely and aimless stroll. But Lily soon realised that they were heading towards the Forest. Why? Why had the Witch brought Lily all the way to the northern border of Selsior?

'Here we are,' the Witch said, sounding pensive. 'Journey's end.'

'What do you mean?' Lily asked.

'This is where we part ways, Lily,' the Witch said sadly. 'My job is now done in Selsior, and my life is coming to an end very soon.'

'How do you know that?' Lily asked. 'Please don't go yet.'

'I do know, Lily, I do,' the Witch said. She paused for a moment. 'Can I confide something in you, Lily?'

'Yes, of course,' Lily said, confused.

'Soon after the rest of the Magical Folk had departed for the Ancient Woodland in the West, I cast a spell tying together my mortality and the freedom of Selsior,' the Witch said.

'Meaning that you wouldn't be able to pass on until the Kingdom was liberated?' Lily asked.

'Yes, that's right,' the Witch said.

'So why did you originally not want to help?' Lily asked, bewildered. 'Why did you not want to help when you would have peace from getting rid of the Goblins?'

'Well, I am not a selfish Witch, Lily – I would not do something just for my own peace!' the Witch said. 'You see, the truth is that over time, I became very bitter and very angry with the Kingdom of Selsior about the way they had treated me and my kind. So when you came, I was telling myself that I would not listen to any petitions from your people... But you wore me down, with your persistence, your *stubbornness*.'

'I try my best!' Lily said, forcing a smile.

'And you impressed me with your cleverness, your curiosity, and your kindness,' the Witch said. 'You showed me that the Kingdom of Selsior would have a bright future indeed if children such as yourself could grow into adulthood in freedom.

'You softened my hard heart, Lily... You made me realise that I had to let go of the past and all of its errors, and instead think about the future and all of its potential. Most importantly, I realised that I could not affect what was behind, but I could affect what was ahead.

'However, I will not be around for that future and for what is ahead. It is time for me to go. I must return to Zelnia.'

'But you can't just leave now!' Lily said pleadingly. 'I spent so much time reading about you, and so much time wanting to meet you, then I find you at last, you rescue Selsior, and now you're just... going!'

'I'm sorry, Lily,' the Witch said, 'but this is the way it has to be.'

'But you don't have to leave *straight away,*' Lily said desperately. 'You must be able to stay a little while. After what you've done? So you can see the Kingdom of Selsior rebuilt?'

'Selsior can now prosper again in peace, but I am no longer needed,' the Witch reiterated. 'And the spell I cast dictates that my time has come.'

'I... I want you to stay...' Lily said as tears rolled down her cheek. She sniffled.

'I know, I know,' the Witch said.

'But... I understand,' Lily said, still tearful and sniffling. 'I understand that you have to go back to Zelnia. I just wish it wasn't so soon...'

The Witch gently wiped the tears from Lily's eyes with her thumb. 'Do not be too upset,' she said. 'Although I am leaving you now, what we have done together will be a story told again and again, until the Veiling of The World.'

'Oh, yes, I am certain of that!' Lily said, smiling – a genuine smile this time.

'So, Lily...' the Witch began, 'here on the southern edge of the Forest, our brief but powerful friendship comes to an end.'

'Before you leave,' Lily said, 'I want to know your name.'

'My real name is lost to history and legend,' the Witch said, 'but you can remember me as "the Last Witch beyond the Forest". And beyond the Forest is where I shall now go, and where I shall rest, forever.'

Lily walked up to the Witch and hugged her tightly, and sniffled again. The Witch returned the embrace for a few moments. Lily let go and took a couple of steps back, wiping another tear.

The Witch held up her hand. Lily wondered what she was doing, when the Witch's broomstick suddenly descended from the air and the Witch grasped it firmly.

'Now I must bid you farewell, courageous Lily,' the Witch said. 'Peacekeeper of Selsior! I know you will fulfil the role marvellously!'

'And I bid the Last Witch beyond the Forest farewell,' Lily said. 'I hope you have a good journey to the other side.'

The Witch got on her broomstick. 'Thank you,' she said. 'I would take another step or two back if I were you.'

Lily took two steps back. The Witch looked at Lily one more time, smiled, and then *whoosh!* The Witch flew through the Forest incredibly fast, to the Land of Zelnia on the other side. Lily looked into the Forest, wiped one last tear from her eye, and then turned to make her way back home.

Lily knocked on the front door of her house. Agatha opened it and gave her daughter a big hug as she came in. Agatha kept one arm around Lily as they walked to the kitchen together.

Agatha had been cooking dinner, while Benjamin, Edwin and Hilary were sitting at the kitchen table with their cutlery ready, just like normal. Lily sat down at the table too, and picked up her knife and fork. She was very excited at the prospect of having a proper meal, after her small snacks in the Forest.

'What's for dinner, Mum?' Edwin asked.

'Well, I've prepared a very special treat for all of us,' Agatha said. 'We are having tomato soup for our starter, then gammon, egg and chips for our main, then chocolate cake for dessert.'

'Oh, that all sounds brilliant!' Lily said blissfully. 'I'm so happy to be back.'

And she really was.

THE END

A. J. Birch is a Creative and Professional Writing graduate of St Mary's University, Twickenham. This is his first novel for children. He lives in Dorking, Surrey.

Printed in Great Britain
by Amazon